NORTHERN REDEMPTION

LAURIE WOOD

More Books in HEROES OF THE TUNDRA Series:
Northern Protector
Northern Hearts
Northern Deception

Merry Christmas Pam & Kevin!

Laurie & Paul Wood

NORTHERN REDEMPTION by LAURIE WOOD

ANAIAH EDGE

An imprint of ANAIAH PRESS, LLC.

7780 49th ST N. #129

Pinellas Park, FL 33781

This book is a work of fiction. All characters, places, names, and events are either a product of the author's imagination or are used fictitiously. Any likeness to any events, locations, or persons, alive or otherwise, is entirely coincidental.

Northern Redemption copyright © 2023 Laurie Wood

All rights reserved, including the right to reproduce this book or portions thereof in any form. For inquiries and information, address Anaiah Press, LLC., 7780 49th ST N. #129 Pinellas Park, Florida, 33781

First Anaiah Edge edition October 2023

Edited by Eden Plantz

Book Design by Anaiah Press

Cover Design by Anaiah Press

In Loving Memory
John Keith Wood
1940-2022
Beloved Dad, Grandpa, Friend

ACKNOWLEDGMENTS

Special thanks go to Paul, my real-life hero who inspires me to keep going on the toughest days! And extra thanks for helping me with the technical details on helicopter piloting and flying in the book. I love you forever and for always.

Special thanks also go to Pat Hanna, private pilot, who gave me photos of small plane crash scenes, along with an owner's manual for a 1968 Piper Arrow. This ensured that the details of my plane crash would be realistic and detailed in the book. I appreciate all your time and input.

To author Ann Brodeur, thank you for your insight and enthusiasm for Lise and Rory's story. Your friendship and critiquing partnership mean everything to me!

To Lynette Stow, another writer friend who's been instrumental in my writing life—I can't thank you enough for teaching a spiritual journaling class at Grant Memorial Baptist Church. You inspired me to write again after I'd given up. Without you, I doubt I'd be published today, so thank you for using your gifts for God's glory.

CHAPTER 1

Friday, October 28
Churchill, Manitoba

A prickle of unease spread down Lise Dumont's spine. She hitched her twelve-gauge shotgun higher on its strap and swung her binoculars eastward. An anonymous caller had reported an adult polar bear out here on Dog Beach, but she hadn't located the bear yet. Curved, bare rocks rose and fell into crevices along the shore of Hudson Bay, stained bright green with decomposing sea kelp.

"See anything?" asked her partner, Braden Scott.

"Not yet."

They'd left their truck on the gravel road and climbed down the rocks to haze the bear out of this zone. They were only two kilometres from town, and tomorrow the children would be out trick-or-treating for Halloween. Every year, bears needed to be kept away from the town limits for people's safety.

She turned to the west and spotted a small pile of dirty white *something* on top of a rock—or behind it.

"Wait, he's about thirty feet over there." She pointed towards the bear and handed Braden the binoculars. "I'll give him a cracker shell and see if he'll move."

Lise ratcheted her shotgun and shot off a blank shell up and over the bear's head. "Anything?" she said.

Braden still stared out his binoculars. "Nothing. Are you sure that's the bear?"

She smiled. "How close do you want to get, rookie?"

"Hey, I defer to your aged wisdom on this one."

"Let's give him another one." Lise took three steps forward and shot to the left of where she could now see the back of the bear. It was an adult male, not impressed with their efforts to make him move from his comfortable bed in the lichen and short willows between the rock bed.

"He's huge. I'll bet he's at least sixteen hundred pounds."

Lise keyed the mic on her radio. "I need the helicopter out here on Dog Beach. I'm going to need to tranquilize this guy for transport to Jail."

"10-4, Lise. Let us know when you've got him down."

"Will do."

"He's standing now." Braden's voice went up a couple of notches. "Man, he is big. Is this their usual size?"

"Males run anywhere from one thousand to seventeen hundred pounds. He's a good size for what we've seen this year," said Lise. "Come back up to the rise and keep him in view with the binocs. I'm going to get the dart gun from the truck."

The polar bear stood, sniffing the afternoon air. He looked almost human as he stood still against the backdrop of the waves rolling in from Hudson Bay. Lise drew in a deep breath as she watched him watching them. The bear was at least twelve feet tall, with paws the size of dinner plates. She noted the long black claws, easily four inches in length. Goose bumps skittered along her arms.

"Don't move, Braden," she said. "If it rushes us, you're going to have to use your shotgun as a club to defend yourself."

"I can't shoot it?"

"You won't have time!" she said. "Stand still."

"Got it." Braden's voice cracked.

Lise eased backwards slowly, never taking her eyes off the bear. She made short work of grabbing the tranquilizer gun when she got to the truck. She took two tranq darts out of the case to make sure she could get the bear immobilized and sedated. She hurried back to Braden's position.

"Okay, I'm going to go around him downwind. You keep watch and tell me if he suddenly changes direction."

"Sure."

Lise smiled at the tremor in Braden's hands on the binoculars. The kid was fresh out of his twenty-week training, and this was his first posting. She'd been brand new three years ago when she'd tranquilized her first bear, which had charged at a tourist who hadn't listened to his tour guide. Had her hands trembled? Probably. She couldn't remember.

The bear dropped to his feet and rubbed his impressive shoulder against the rocks. Lise looked through her scope and took careful aim at his other shoulder, where it joined his neck. She held her breath and squeezed the trigger. The dart flew and hit its target. The bear ran a couple of steps forward, then turned in a circle, then back towards them, the orange dart sticking out of his neck.

"You did it!" Braden whooped.

"I should've made you do it," Lise called back to him. "He's going to sleep now."

The bear collapsed like a boneless puppet, all dirty, white, spiky fur. His tongue stuck out a few inches to the left. Lise realized she was holding her breath. The bear seemed even bigger now that he had relaxed in his drugged state. The *whop-whop-whop* of the helicopter blades coming down the bay sounded like victory.

"Let's get him ready for transport," she yelled to Braden. "Bring me the net from the truck."

Braden waved and turned to run back over the rocks to the truck. The yellow helicopter hovered over her, the rotors pushing air downwards and whipping up the water against the rocks. The whoosh of air made her ponytail fly in all directions and lashed her hair around her eyes. She shaded them with one hand and peered up at the pilot causing her hair distress. It looked like Rory Gallagher from Northern Lights Tours, but she couldn't be sure. Maybe it was Jack McIssac.

The pilot waved at her with a smirk and then pulled the helicopter ahead to hover over the bear's inert form. Braden appeared with the heavy net and tackle, breathing hard after climbing down the rocks. She turned her attention to the young rookie.

"All right, we're going to put this black cloth over its eyes to protect them," she said as they walked up to the huge male bear flopped over on his side. "Then we're going to put down the net and roll him on to the middle of it."

She took the black strip of cloth from Braden and deftly tied it around the top of the bear's head, covering its eyes. Her movements were sure and strong.

"How are we going to get him in the middle of the net?" Braden's voice could barely be heard over the noise of the helicopter rotors above them. "He's dead weight."

Lise took one side of the net and pointed to the end of the same side, motioning for Braden to pick it up. They each pulled forward, away from the bear, until she put her hand up in a "stop" motion.

"Okay, now we roll him onto the edge of the net, and once we roll him over, then we can spread it out on the other side. Then, we bring all four corners together to hook the tackle up securely to the cable the helicopter is going to send down."

Despite the bear's weight, it was easy to roll him over. His muscles were as loose as jelly. Lise grabbed two corners and motioned for Braden to grab the other two corners. Bringing them together, she waved at the helicopter to lower the cable to her. She put the huge hook through the four metal circles on each corner of the net and let Braden double-check that the hook was secure. They stepped back out of the way, and she twirled her right hand in the air to show the pilot he was free to raise the bear in the air and take off.

The pilot saluted them as the helicopter rose, the netted bear suspended underneath. The downdraft still messed with her hair, and she shoved her curls out of her eyes so she could watch the magnificent animal being flown south out of town to the Polar Bear Holding Facility, known locally as the Polar Bear Jail.

"Wow, that was really something," said Braden. "I've never been that up close to a dangerous animal before."

"And that's the closest you want to get to a polar bear," Lise said. "He could've charged us. We got lucky that time." She headed up the rocks to their truck. "Let's go meet him at the Jail. He can rest with the others for the next month."

Braden climbed into their 4x4 Conservation truck as Lise started the engine. She drove over the rutted gravel road that ran along the rock way down to the beach area. It wasn't a beach in the genuine sense of the word. Up here, *beach* meant where the stony edge of land met the waters of Hudson Bay. Rivulets of sand kissed the water, but the beach was mostly layers of flat rocks, worn down from generations of waves rolling over them.

"I'm glad you're back, but does this mean Steve Old will be leaving?" asked Braden. His left knee jumped up and down, and she watched his hand clench and unclench on his thigh.

She smiled. A normal reaction to being within twenty feet of a gigantic polar bear.

"He's due to rotate out anyway, but he's being promoted to a supervisor position. It'll be you and I for the next two years." She paused. "If I decide to stay."

Braden whipped his head around. "You have a choice? I thought you were back for good. Weren't you on leave or something?"

Lise gripped the steering wheel, her knuckles turning white. "Or something" was right. Something she didn't feel like talking about with this twenty-four-year-old rookie.

"I took a temporary leave because I was getting married down south. I wanted to look over my options, career-wise." Her cell phone vibrated on the dashboard, showing the number for her best friend, Kira Tanner. Kira had staying power, that was for sure. She never took no for an answer.

"Not my business, but did you get married?" Braden's knee still jumped, but when she glanced down, she noticed his fist remained clenched on top of it.

"Do you see a wedding ring anywhere?" She couldn't keep the bitterness out of her voice. Stupid. Not the kid's fault. "Sorry. It's not something I like to talk about."

"No, I'm sorry. It's not my business."

"You're right. And I don't talk about it." She turned to stare at him. "Men aren't at the top of my hit parade right now."

Braden nodded like a bobblehead. "Got it. Being a man, I'll try to keep that in mind."

She huffed out a laugh. "No worries, kid. I consider you more like a little brother."

She swung the truck up the driveway to the Polar Bear Jail, a rounded metal building that the military once used back in the 1960s. The side of the building facing the main highway was painted with a mural of a giant sleeping polar bear.

They jumped out of the truck as the helicopter swung wide around the top of the building and began hovering over the front drive. The Jail employed two workers who watched over any bears in house. George Fleming drove an ATV with a flat wooden trailer out of the main doors. Lise and Braden jumped out and ran to the ATV as the helicopter swayed above them.

Lise waved her right arm, directing the pilot as he hovered over the trailer. The bear was still about fifty feet in the air. The helicopter started going back up instead of lowering down. She jumped up and down, trying to catch the pilot's attention. The netted bear swayed side to side as the helicopter rose higher.

Lise ran to her truck and grabbed her radio off the dashboard. "RCMP dispatch, come in."

"Dispatch, go ahead." Trudy's calm voice came over the air.

"We've got a problem with the helicopter out here at the Polar Bear Jail. I don't know what's going on, but it looks like he's got a control issue. Send me some help."

"What do you need? Have you tried his radio?"

"No, the chopper's going back up, and it doesn't look like he's able to keep the bear steady. I don't know what he's doing."

"I'll try and radio him," said Trudy.

"Okay." Lise shaded her eyes and tracked the chopper moving to the right, away from the trailer.

"Hey, Lise," Trudy broke into her thoughts, "he says he's had some radio issues too, and I'm going to send out the works. Keep trying him on channel two."

"Right, channel two." Lise's stomach clenched as the bear

in the net swung wide at the end of its wire rope. If it kept swinging too far in a circle, it would disturb the helicopter's equilibrium.

"10-4, Lise. I'm sending police, fire, and ambulance now."

"10-4." Lise stared into the sky.

The pilot abruptly flew sideways to the right and looked like he was coming back to try again. She'd flown in helicopters a hundred times as part of the job. She'd never seen a pilot do these kinds of manoeuvres before.

Lise's stomach bottomed out as she watched the pilot coming straight towards them. Something was terribly wrong. And that bear would wake up any minute. If the pilot couldn't land, it would panic and tear the net to shreds. Then, it would plunge to its death. Her heart pounded in her ears as she willed the pilot to keep the helicopter in the air. The last thing she wanted on her conscience was a dead bear and pilot.

Please, Lord, help him get it under control, she prayed. *Please.*

Rory Gallagher had flown thousands of hours in this model of helicopter. He'd bought this one only two years ago. He tried to push down on the collective to his left, trying unsuccessfully to lower the helicopter towards the trailer below. The bear moved its front paws in the net as it swayed in his side window. He punched the window with his left fist.

Burning anger flushed his face, turning his skin as red as his hair. This wasn't supposed to happen. He couldn't land if the collective wouldn't release and let him lower the helicopter.

Thank heavens the malfunction hadn't happened with three clients on board for a tour. On the other hand, he knew if that bear fell to the ground and died, this would be the last time the Conservation Office hired him to do a bear run.

He gave up on the collective and pushed his cyclic—or joystick, as civilians liked to call it—from side to side to tilt the rotors above him to change direction away from the jail site. If he ended up dropping the bear, he wanted it to land on a grassy, if frozen, area of the tundra, and maybe the animal would have a chance of survival.

"JR one to base," he radioed. Jack McIsaac better be in the office by now.

"Base, go ahead." Relief at the sound of Jack's voice flooded his nervous system.

"I've got a problem with the collective. It's seized up, and I can't land with this bear. Call RCMP and Fire for a probable crash landing."

"Are you sure, boss?" Jack's voice shrilled through the radio.

"As sure as I'm going to be a smoking hole in the ground if we don't figure this out."

"Calling them now. Stand by."

Rory checked his fuel gauge. Half a tank left. So, he could fly until he ran out of fuel, or he could crash land with enough to blow himself up. Or he could try to shut off his engine and hope pointing straight down would give him enough air lift on his rotors as he crashed to cushion his landing.

"JR one, come in." A female voice he didn't recognize. Someone new at the RCMP detachment?

"JR one, I'm a little busy up here."

"Police, fire, and ambo are standing by here. What's your plan?" She sounded in control but younger than Trudy, who'd been working at the detachment for the past twenty years.

"My plan is to survive, lady. Is Ben Koper on site?"

Ben Koper was one of the town's RCMP officers and Rory's brother-in-law. Right now, he wanted to talk to family.

"He's been notified of your situation, and he's on his way. Do you want to talk to anyone else?"

"Negative." He peeked out his left side window and saw the bear moving its hind legs now. Great.

"Let's talk options, JR one." She was bossy with a hard edge to her voice. Who the heck was this?

"Not too many options available." His voice rose as he banked again to come around from the back of the jail. "I can fly till I run out of fuel, which will take about three-quarters of an hour."

"Then you'll crash, right?" Now, her voice showed some strain. Good. He didn't want to be the only one concerned about his imminent death.

"Affirmative."

"Anything else? There must be something you can do." Her intense voice filled the cabin. "Give me another option."

He laughed. "Lady, I'd love to tell you I'm not going to flame out of the sky or kill this bear, but I don't know what's going to happen here."

"You're the expert. Think of something. What's wrong with the helicopter, anyway?"

"In layman's terms, I can't move the lever that makes the helicopter lower so I can land. It's seized up. If I can't land, I can only flame out or shut off my engine and pray my rotors will help cushion the landing."

"Have you ever done that before?" she asked. Maybe this was the Conservation Officer?

"We train for it, but I've never done it with a sixteen-hundred-pound bear attached to me. I've got to go higher."

"Then get higher. I saw you doing that before this last try. Go higher."

Who was this overbearing woman?

"What about the bear? I'm trying to stay close to the

ground in case he falls out of the net. If I go higher, he could die in a fall."

The silence spread for so long that he thought he'd lost her.

"The bear is important, but you're more important. *Please.* Save yourself."

He cleared his throat. Sweat plastered his shirt to his back, and heat flushed through his body again. "Did you say fire and ambulance are standing by?"

Silence.

"They're both here. Do what you need to do to save yourself. We're all here rooting for you."

Okay. He sucked in a deep breath. This was it. He had one shot at making the landing work. He banked the helicopter around again to line up with the wide field area beside the jail. He pulled up on the collective to rise in the air, feeling the weight of the netted bear still on the end of the cable. They rose into the air, and he held the helicopter as straight as he could, fighting the extra weight of the bear.

He didn't know what shape the bear was in, but he needed to land this helicopter. Now, when he pushed hard down on the collective, it released, letting him descend. He could hear clicking and cheers over his radio. He blew out his breath and shook his head to clear it.

Gently moving the collective up and down, he brought the helicopter to hover over the wooden trailer outside of the jail. Then he descended farther until the bear lay on top of the plywood trailer. He could see people jumping up and down and waving at him.

"JR one, come in." Great. His bossy lady was back again.

"Hey. How's the bear?"

"I'll check him in a minute. How are you?" She sounded breathless now.

"Afraid to land this puppy."

"You can do it. Emergency services are right here."

"Thanks for the vote of confidence," he said.

He stared down at the redhead in the Conservation Officer uniform. He'd been right, then. Nice of her to keep him talking through the worst of it. She twirled her right hand in the air at him, and he realized they'd moved the bear on the trailer out from underneath him.

The helicopter still hovered in place, but he said a prayer under his breath to the God he didn't believe in as he put his hand on the collective again.

"Okay, God, let's do this," he muttered, "and try not to end up in a fiery crater."

He eased the collective down slowly, his right hand on the cyclic, while working his feet on the controls. The helicopter dropped abruptly, then responded to his touch and lowered to the ground. He blew out another breath when he felt the runners hit the rough sedge grass to the left of the driveway. He reached up and turned off the rotors, which slowed and came to a stop.

Well, that was fun. A sharp rapping on his plexiglass door made him jump.

"Are you alright?" The young woman's hair whipped around her head in the rotor wash. Was her skin always that pale, or was she scared? The freckles across her nose and cheeks were cute. Wait, he was noticing freckles? Maybe he was oxygen-deprived.

"I'm fine," he said as he took off his headset and motioned to her to move away from the door. He could see people standing around the fire truck. Their emergency lights flashed red strobes on the snow, as did the RCMP car that was pulling in. Probably Ben, racing out here from home.

He pushed open the door and jumped down onto the ground. Yes, his legs wobbled in the knees. Not that he was about to tell anyone that, and certainly not this attractive woman with the frosty blue eyes and mass of tangled red hair.

"You should let the EMTs check you out. That was scary. You could've crashed." She made a move towards him as if to hug him. She stopped herself, rocking back and forth in her boots. A slow blush rose over her cheeks. She dipped her head down.

"I'm fine. Seriously." He wanted to take hold of the tip of that chin and tilt her face up. What he'd give to see those amazing blue eyes again.

Ben Koper hurried up and punched him in the shoulder. "You nearly scared us to death. Joy's going to want a full report. You okay?"

Seriously, bro, could you have any worse timing?

"Yeah, it's the helicopter that's whacked. One of my maintenance guys must've messed up, or maybe there's a part broken in the collective mechanism. I'm going to leave it here and get the guys out to look at it. I didn't want to chance a crash at the airport and tie up their resources."

Ben grinned. "I told Joy you'd have everything in hand, but you know your sister. And I'd better tell dispatch to call your mom as well." He turned to head back to his cruiser. He waved over his shoulder. "Glad you're okay, man."

Rory accepted the congratulations of the volunteer firefighters and EMTs. He watched the red-headed conservation officer back away and then head to her truck out of the corner of his eye. The guys were laughing and yelling when he tried to tell her to stay. He'd seen her before, from a distance, but not for months. What was her story? He figured he could ask his sister once he got back into town.

The bear was gone, so they must've taken him inside. He stared at the redhead driving away in the truck with some young guy in the passenger seat. The woman on the radio didn't sound like someone who would run away. He wanted to thank her for keeping him focused up there. Maybe they'd gotten another call.

Shivers ran up and down his body as his adrenaline settled down. He'd find and thank her somehow. Surely, a woman who confronted polar bears every day wasn't afraid of a little conversation.

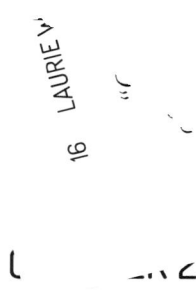

Late the next afternoon, Lise entered the small Conservation office at the back of the Town Centre. Her phone was blowing up with texts from both Aidan and her mother.

Your father and I are concerned about you. Aidan says he has no idea where you are... call us, please!

You think this is some kind of sick joke? You think you can make a fool out of me? Call me NOW, or you'll be sorry!

She couldn't shut her phone off. She needed the cell for work. Her parents she could deal with later. Only three weeks had passed since she'd fled Winnipeg. Aidan's texts had escalated, though. Her stomach curdled. She'd seen glimpses of rage in his eyes before but never as shocking as when he'd grabbed her arm.

"What do you mean, you haven't sent in your resignation for that stupid job? I told you to do that a month ago." He squeezed her bicep like an orange. She gasped as he pulled her towards his face. "You're going to have all the money you ever wanted, marrying me."

"You're hurting me!" Her breath stopped; the room tilted sideways. "Let go of me, now."

*r what? Where do you think you're going to go?" He let go her so fast her knees went out from under her. "You have nothing of your own here in Winnipeg. And nothing but a dingy apartment in Churchill. You're out of options. And when you become Mrs. Aidan Grant, I expect you to follow through when I tell you to do something."

He'd walked away from her, confident she would do what she was told and serve him dinner in their downtown condo. Instead, she'd run out to the elevator, down to her car, and driven straight to the airport.

What's wrong with me? Why didn't I see it sooner?

She pocketed her phone and stood in the doorway and took a few deep breaths. She was two thousand kilometres away from him. He could text all he wanted. She was safe up here.

Braden was working at his computer, and their dispatcher, Denise Watchorn, pointed at a colourful bouquet on Lise's desk.

"Those came for you this morning," she said, her computer glasses riding down on her nose. "I didn't open the card."

Lise grimaced as she hung up her dark green parka. "Those had better not be from who I think they're from," she said. Her stomach roiled again. The last thing she needed was Aiden love-bombing her from afar. She needed time and space to clear her head. Without thinking, she massaged her left bicep where he'd grabbed her that night. The bruise had faded to a sickly green, but her memory of that night was in technicolour.

"There's no special occasion?" said Denise.

Lise knew her friend meant well. She also knew everyone in town was dying to know where the two-carat diamond had gone from her left hand and why she'd suddenly shown up three weeks ago asking Steve Olds for her job back. And she still owed her best friend, Kira Tanner, a proper phone call.

She pulled the green tissue paper down from around the

cut flowers in a glass vase. True to her word, Denise had left the card unopened. Flying flowers up here would've cost a fortune. Typical Aidan. In the weeks since she'd last seen him, she now realized he'd pick a fight and then send an enormous bouquet to "make up" and expect instant forgiveness. Something else she'd never figured out till this minute.

Flipping the card open with her thumbnail, she read the words in disbelief. Not Aidan.

Thanks for being the voice of common sense yesterday. You were a lifesaver.

Rory Gallagher.

Lise sucked in a dazed breath. She shoved the card back into the envelope and then down into her pants pocket. *Rory Gallagher.* The only thing she knew about him was that he was a confirmed bachelor who lived outside of town and avoided people who weren't paying tourists.

And had the same flame-red hair she did, along with the deep amber-hazel eyes that had bored into her yesterday after he nearly crashed and burned. His chin stubble and moustache were the antitheses of Aidan's pampered skin.

She leaned in to smell the gorgeous dahlias, carnations, mini roses, and daisies. They burst with brilliant oranges, yellows, and scarlet. Rory had spent a few hundred dollars, at least. She'd only done what anyone would've done—even though she was the only one there to take control of the situation, Braden being brand new off the plane from Winnipeg.

The flowers smelled of sunshine, fall air, and the south. All things she'd come up here to run away from, but she inhaled deeply again one more time.

"Aren't you going to tell us who your secret admirer is?" Denise clasped her hands together and leaned forward, her elbows on her desk. "This is more excitement than we had all summer."

"Nope, the secret stays with me," said Lise. Her hands shook, and she shoved them in her front pockets. "Now, what's happening with the bear monitors for Halloween tonight? Do we have enough volunteers?"

Denise sighed dramatically at the change in subject. "Not really. We're missing a few regulars." She pushed her glasses up her nose and peered at her computer. "Lukas Tanner and his assistant, Ezra Reimer, volunteered this year. And Ben Koper, over at the RCMP detachment, said he, Adam, and Zack will all be out tonight as well."

"We'll have to start early then," said Lise. "Braden, you and I can patrol out along the shoreline from here to Dog Beach again. We'll have everyone on the same radio frequency."

"Okay." He kept typing into his computer. "The bear traps around the perimeter are all filled with seal bait and ready to go."

"We'll start patrolling any time. The kids usually start trick-or-treating by 4:00 p.m. and then end up at The Great Northern Lodge with their parents for a party by 5:30 p.m. We still need to be out there patrolling, though, for the older kids who go partying from house to house."

"There's supposed to be snow coming in tonight or tomorrow. We haven't had a storm yet this season," said Braden.

"Don't start saying that or you'll bring one on for sure," said Denise. "Usually, we only have freezing cold on Halloween."

Lise checked the weather maps on her own computer. She tapped her teeth with her pen. "Says here polar air is coming down next week. Maybe a chance of a blizzard with a ridge of snow coming in from the west."

"Do kids really go outside to trick-or-treat when it's -26 Celsius?" asked Braden.

"This is all they know, so yes, if it means free candy, of

course they do," said Denise. "Back in the day, my kids would go out if it was -35 Celsius."

Lise touched the petals of a huge orange dahlia, the sounds of Braden and Denise chattering floating over her head. The flowers made her uncomfortable, but she couldn't put her finger on why. Surely, Rory didn't have any expectations. Usually, when a man gave a woman this enormous a bouquet, they had an emotional connection.

It's a thank you, nothing more.

"Guys, I'm going to grab some coffee over at Ruby's. Do either of you want anything?" Lise jumped to her feet and grabbed her parka from the rack. She hadn't seen Ruby yet, and if anyone knew how to solve problems, she did.

"Not for me," said Denise. "I'll never sleep tonight."

"I'll wait for you here," said Braden.

Lise shoved open the door and went out into frigid air that bit into her cheeks. *This* was what she'd missed so much. Their office faced the frozen, grassy slope heading down to the back gravel road that circled the town along the shoreline. She could see the choppy green-grey waves of water roaring in for the late tide. The vast expanse of Hudson Bay unrolled before her, lifting her confined spirit and soothing her soul.

She could walk the long way around to get to Ruby's Café and Emporium, but being bear season, one could meet a bear anywhere at any time. She headed to her work truck and started the engine. Better safe than sorry. No one walked except in large groups, and the children tonight would have adult escorts armed with bear deterrents.

Lise swung the truck around the far corner of the Town Centre and hoped Ruby wasn't too busy for a cup of coffee. Her own mother adored Aidan. Would she even believe he'd assaulted her? Ruby always knew the right things to say. She gunned the motor and took off down Kelsey Boulevard.

Her cell phone rang beside her on the truck seat. Kira again. She picked up the phone and swiped right.

"Hey, I'm working," she raised her voice above the noise of the truck.

"Hey, yourself. Joy wants to know if you can join us and the girls to go trick-or-treating tonight. When do you get off work?" Kira's upbeat voice filled the truck cab.

"We don't get off till all the partiers are at home, but I'd love to see the girls in their costumes. Maybe I can swing by Joy's place in a bit."

"Great! Emberlyn is dying to show off her warrior princess costume."

"What's Sophie going to be this year?" asked Lise. She heard giggling and screeches in the background.

"She's a fairy princess. Everyone's a princess," said Kira. "She's absolutely adorable, in my completely unbiased opinion."

"Okay, I've got to go, but I'll swing by later."

"See you! And we still need to talk," said Kira.

"Yeah, just not tonight." Lise parked in front of the Café and turned off the truck. They had decorated the huge front window with spiders and carved pumpkin graphics, and orange LED lights surrounded the edges of it. Ruby always loved to decorate for the season.

"I'm here when you need me," said Kira.

"I know, my friend. Gotta go." Lise hung up and stretched inside the truck.

She and Kira had been fast friends since she'd been a rookie up here three years ago. She knew Kira meant well—everyone did—but she wasn't ready to talk about Aidan and the mess she'd made of her life down south. Kira and Lukas were a classic love story. They'd found each other again after being college sweethearts. She and Aidan? Not so classic.

She flexed her fingers and looked at the blank spot on her left hand where her engagement ring had been. Aidan had swept her off her feet over a year ago. He'd been up here on a summer tour with his manager, looking to invest in the Arctic. They'd literally run into each other going into The Great Northern Lodge and Restaurant, and he'd asked her if she was local. Then he'd asked her to dinner.

After that, they'd flown on chartered planes, both back to Winnipeg and to the United States, taking in his business ventures. Then, to Europe and its capital cities. She'd juggled her vacation time, sick days, and an unpaid leave of absence to be with him. Finally, Steve Olds told her she needed to choose —her career or her relationship. And she thought she'd chosen Aidan.

Lise climbed out of the truck and left the doors unlocked. Locking one's vehicles or doors was illegal in Churchill in case someone needed to escape from a wandering bear in town. She laughed to herself as she went up the stairs to the Café. How fast she'd gotten back into the rhythm of life up north.

The sweet smell of cinnamon buns and pie wafted across the Café in the warm air. Multiple voices rose around her as she walked over to the main counter. Ruby had switched things up a bit since she'd been gone. More banks of tables ran along the walls, with tall risers in between for privacy. The "gossip" table was still over to the left, where the old-timers liked to congregate and spend a few hours with their coffees to play Hearts. And she noticed that the clothing racks on the Emporium side had expanded.

"Lise, it is you! How're you doing, my girl?" Ruby's brown eyes sparked with warmth as she finished wiping down the counter. "Sit, sit. What kind of pie would you like? It's on the house."

"That's so kind of you, Ruby." Lise sat on one of the red

stools at the counter. "I see you've done it up right for Halloween this year." She pointed at the gauzy white filament hanging from the ceiling and lining the back shelves behind the counter. Homemade black paper spiders hung down as well.

"The grade four kids brought those spiders over the other day. Their poor teacher had to do something with them to keep them from climbing the walls. They were so excited."

"I remember loving trick-or-treating when I was a kid," said Lise. "It was all about the candy and treats."

"Perfectly harmless," said Ruby. "Now, what kind of pie, m'dear?"

"This time of year, you must have some pumpkin," said Lise. "I'd love a piece of that or whatever you've got the most of. I'm not picky."

"Pumpkin it is. Wait, and I'll grab the whipped cream." Ruby disappeared into the back kitchen.

"Coffee?" asked a Nordic blonde girl whom Lise had never seen before. She held the pot over the mug next to Lise.

"Sure, thank you." Lise took a couple of sugar packs and creamers off the carousel to her right. Ruby bustled back with a plate of pie topped four inches high with whipped cream.

"Oh, my word, Ruby." Lise's eyes pricked with tears. Her throat closed, and for a second, she thought she'd burst out ugly crying. *I'm such a mess. What's wrong with me?* She ducked her head so no one would see the tears standing in her eyes. Not quick enough, because Ruby reached out and took her by the hands.

"It's going to be okay." Ruby squeezed her hands tight and then released her. Her empathy enveloped Lise like a warm hug. "Whatever it is, it's going to be okay."

"Coffee and pie can solve anything, right?" Lise picked up her fork, her voice wobbling.

"Not everything, but good friends and time can certainly

help." Ruby resumed putting napkins in the metal napkin holders, giving Lise space to eat her pie. "And this place can give a person the proper perspective if you know what I mean."

Her emotions crumbled inside her, but the pie melted in her mouth, and the coffee tasted like heaven. She felt like she had come home, which was weird because her tiny apartment felt like anything but home. Maybe that was part of the problem. Where and what was home?

"Perspective is exactly what I need." Lise forked another bite of pie into her mouth. "How do you get over making the biggest mistake of your life?"

Ruby reached over and patted Lise's left hand, where the monstrous engagement ring was missing. "Your heart knows the truth. Trust your heart because that's really God telling you what to do. If you took off that ring, you did it for a good reason, m'dear."

Lise picked up her coffee mug to hide her trembling lips. "It was a good reason, but I don't think my mother will understand."

She remembered her mother's pride at their engagement party when her father announced their new address in an exclusive area of Winnipeg. Aidan had a downtown Toronto condo as well, with another one facing the ocean in Vancouver. She'd given up the life of a rich woman. But what would the cost have been to her own selfhood and safety if she'd gone through with the wedding?

Ruby squeezed her hand. "It's your life, not your mother's. She'll understand in time."

Ruby poured herself a cup of coffee. "I heard you helped my son land yesterday."

Lise laughed for the first time since she'd gotten off the plane out at the airport three weeks ago. "No good deed goes unpunished. I bet you heard about it before I was even back in town last night."

Ruby smiled over the rim of her mug. "Eh, I have my sources. Thank you for keeping a cool head about you. I guess air traffic control let you talk him through it."

"Did your sources tell you Rory sent me a bouquet as a thank you?" As soon as she said the words, she regretted them. She should've kept his gift a secret. She suddenly wanted to talk to Rory about the flowers, not his mom. She wiped her mouth with a napkin.

Ruby regarded her with a quirked eyebrow. "I guess my sources aren't as good as I thought they were." She leaned on the counter. "But if he sent you flowers, it's a thank you, nothing more."

Lise nodded. Of course, that was all they were, a thank you. She had zero interest in dealing with any male attention. Her primary goal was unpacking what had happened with Aidan and how to avoid making the same mistake twice. And a guy who sent enormous bouquets worth hundreds of dollars as a grand gesture was another mistake waiting to happen.

"I've got to get back to work." She pulled her parka back on. "Thanks so much, Ruby."

"My pleasure, my girl. Come in any time." Ruby took the dirty dishes and beamed at her. "I'm glad you're back where you belong."

Lise whipped her head back and forth outside on the front deck, checking for bears before heading to her truck. *Back where you belong.*

Did she belong up here? She'd thought she loved Aidan so much she could give all this up. Still, she missed the excitement of taking care of the polar bears and multitude of wildlife in the Wildlife Management Area. Patrolling Wapusk National Park forty-five kilometres to the south of

Churchill. She'd adored every minute of her job before she met Aidan.

He'd turned up his nose at her apartment and complained about the poor fare and amenities at the various hotels in town. He'd tried them all, saying he was looking to invest, but in the end, he'd decided against doing any business in the town. Nothing met his standards. Good thing she'd discovered at the eleventh hour before their wedding that she didn't meet his standards either.

Pulling up outside Joy and Ben Koper's townhouse, she closed her eyes and took a deep breath. She would not think that way. She *was* enough. She moved her arm and remembered the rage in his eyes as he grabbed her and swung her around. If Ben knew her story, she already knew what he would tell her.

Emberlyn appeared in the living room window, jumping up and down, waving and yelling. She smiled. Nothing like the power of children's joy to bring one out of the doldrums. She headed in to see her friends.

Rory stood by his living room window, watching the rose and gold of the sun's late afternoon rays play against the bluish white of the snow. He loved the quiet of living out of town, surrounded by endless kilometres of flat rocks, stunted trees, and rolling tundra.

Dressed in his work uniform of flannel-lined cargo pants, long-sleeve T-shirt, and blue plaid flannel shirt over top, he sipped a cup of coffee. Halloween night bear patrol usually ran late, so he'd grabbed an extra caffeine hit and was almost ready to head out.

He strode over to his oak bookcase, which held wooden

watch cases of ten watches each. Each shelf held three cases side by side. He mulled over which watch he felt like wearing tonight. Collecting watches was his passion. He belonged to several online groups catering to collectors all over the world.

The top of the bookcase held his favourite watches, the ones he wore and rotated through the most often. He loved the robustness of dive watches, even though Churchill was far from any tropical diving climates.

One green field watch stood out with its broken crystal and its hands stopped at the one and the eight. He caressed the ragged edges of the crystal with a fingertip. His dad had worn this watch the day he drowned in the Churchill River seven years ago. Rory couldn't bear to get the keepsake fixed. He knew an excellent watchmaker in Winnipeg, but it felt wrong to change the time of his father's death, as if he would somehow be dishonouring his father.

His life had stood still in some ways, the same as the watch had, but he didn't dwell on it. He hadn't been able to save his father, and he expected nothing good from life once his beloved role model had been taken from him.

His hand hovered over a blue diver and a grey field watch from World War II. He might be wrestling with bears or drunk partiers tonight, so he picked the diver because it wasn't vintage. The blue dial matched the dark blue stripe in his flannel shirt.

He laughed to himself as he put the watch on his left wrist. "Must make sure everything matches, eh Bosco?" he asked his elegant grey Persian cat, who was purring madly on the back of the leather recliner. He rubbed the feline's fat cheeks and petted its head. "Even you match my colour scheme. Joy would never let me forget it if she ever came out here to visit us."

He'd adopted four-year-old Bosco from a rescue in southern Manitoba. Unlike every other male friend he had, Rory didn't own a dog. Growing up, his parents had no time for pets, and he saw them more as working animals.

One night he had been scrolling online through rescue groups, thinking *maybe* he would get a dog, seeing as he lived almost out at the airport, when he spotted Bosco's photo. The young cat had melted his heart and was on the next plane up north. Bosco listened to him without comment, enjoyed Rory's company when he wanted it, and didn't ask to be taken outside or exercised. Bosco was the perfect companion.

"Gotta go to work, Bozz," said Rory as he pulled on his mukluks. He shoved his arms into his parka and made sure his heavy gloves were in the pockets. "Guard the place while I'm gone."

He laughed to himself at his own joke as he headed out to his truck. He probably should get a guard dog living out here alone, about twenty-three kilometres from town, but he'd never felt the need.

As he pulled onto the road from his long driveway, he wondered what Lise had thought of the flowers and if they'd arrived fresh enough. Like adopting Bosco, he'd ordered the bouquet during the night, on impulse, while scrolling through social media. The decision had been reckless, and he hoped she didn't make too much out of the gesture. He and Bosco did fine on their own.

Twenty minutes later, he pulled up outside of Joy's townhouse and could see a knot of children and adults already at one end of the block. He left his truck on the opposite side of the road and left the doors unlocked. He brought out his bear horn, bear spray, and slid his 12-gauge shotgun, loaded with cracker shells, over his shoulder on its strap.

Emberlyn came racing down the stairs of the townhouse porch towards him, her red and gold costume over her parka sparkling in the late afternoon light.

"Uncle Rory! You came. See my sword?" Her feet shuddered to a stop in front of him. She waved a plastic sword in his face. "I'm a warrior princess. I fight for my people against the evil queen, Morgaine."

He laughed out loud. Her plastic gold crown sat askew on her head, but he admired her for not caring that her princess dress was three sizes too big because it had to go over her parka and snow pants. The fake red and gold brocade strained against the zipper of her coat. Joy had braided her hair and then made buns out of the braids around her ears.

He bowed low to her. "My princess! That is a serious sword you have there. I hope I never have to feel the wrath of your blade."

Emberlyn burst into giggles. She touched him with the sword on either shoulder as he stayed bowed over. "You are Sir Rory, the Knight of Ice and Frost. You may be my guard."

"I *am* your guard, little one. Where's your mom?"

"She's talking to Kira and some red-haired lady over there." Emberlyn pointed behind her. "See Sophie? She's a princess, too. And my friend Jacinthe from school. We're all princesses this year." She turned and ran back towards her mother. "Mom! Uncle Rory's here. We can start now."

Rory stared down the row of townhouses and spotted Lise standing among the group of women and children. Her blazing red hair stood out against the dull, painted wooden sides of the buildings. Why wasn't she wearing a hat? She hadn't worn one yesterday, either. She must not mind the cold on the ears. His ears would be frostbitten in minutes if he didn't wear a toque.

Ben came out of his house and down the few stairs to shake hands with him. "Good to have an extra body on duty tonight. Trudy just called me. We've gotten a notice that two escapees have broken out of jail in Thompson."

"They're not likely to come this far north," said Rory.

"D'you think? Wouldn't they try to head south and get lost in a big city like Winnipeg?"

"Probably, but now I've got to send the guys over to the train station to check everyone coming off the train tonight. Just to be sure." Ben sighed as he fastened his gloves on.

"I can be wherever you need me." Rory glanced down the row again and kept Lise within eyesight. Ben followed his gaze.

"There's a story there, but Joy hasn't unloaded it yet," said Ben.

"She was barely working here, and then she was gone." Rory shifted his shotgun on his shoulder. "I thought you'd hired a new constable when I heard her on the radio yesterday."

"Well, she's back for some reason," said Ben. He jerked his chin towards Lise. "She may need a partner if Steve Olds takes out the rookie."

Rory blushed a ferocious red. This was why he was still single. His own traitorous body fought against him. Ben clapped him on the shoulder.

"Hey, it's bear monitoring, not a lifetime commitment." Ben headed past him to his own RCMP truck. "See you all later. Stay on channel two."

"See you," said Rory, as Emberlyn, Sophie Tanner, and a gaggle of children in superhero, princess, and animal costumes came running down the communal deck of the townhouses. Apparently, they'd finished with this row and were ready to go on to the next one.

The three women walked up to him, his sister Joy grinning like a Jack-o'-lantern.

"Hey, Rory." She kissed him on the cheek. "I'm so glad you managed not to end up in a blaze of glory yesterday." She hugged him hard.

He returned the hug, looking at Lise over Joy's shoulder. Rarely did he find a woman as tall as he was, never mind one carrying a shotgun over her shoulder. She stood so close he could smell the lilac scent of her shampoo.

"You're going to need a hat tonight," he blurted out, releasing Joy.

Joy laughed and punched him in the shoulder. She covered up his gaffe by saying, "My brother's right, it's going down to -29C. Where's your hat?"

"Left it in the truck." Lise stared at him while he writhed inside from blushing. "Um, I need to get back to the office."

Could the icy road open up and swallow him whole? Living up north meant living free, but it also meant a lack of social graces with the opposite sex. He hadn't had an actual relationship since right before his dad died. Given his stupid comment just now, he didn't deserve an actual relationship.

"I'm supposed to be one of your bear monitors." His blood pounded in his ears. He should've told Ben he'd go with the guys over to the train station.

"Oh." Her eyes widened. She looked at Joy as if for help. "Sure. We need a ton of help. Can you patrol in town, or do you want to do the shoreline?"

"Why don't the two of you ride together?" asked Joy.

"I can do town..." Rory shot a furious look at his sister.

"Aren't you supposed to double up in case you come in contact with a bear?" said Kira. Sophie pulled on her mother's hand. "Sophie, wait a sec. We'll be done in a minute."

A raucous chorus of horns blared from someone's truck. The women shrieked and grabbed their children as a polar bear cub flashed down the street, followed by a black pickup truck. Everyone raced up the stairs to the common area of the deck and watched the truck haze the baby bear down the rest of the street and around the corner at the bottom.

A police siren sounded over one street on its way back towards them.

"That's probably Ben," said Joy. "We should stay inside until he calls me. The mother bear can't be too far behind."

She ushered the small crowd through her townhouse door. Rory and Lise stood inside the foyer as the children burst into the living room.

"I really need to get out there," Lise said. "Steve will be having fits."

"Joy's right, you need a partner."

"I'm supposed to be training Braden." She took her radio mic off her shoulder epaulet. "Dispatch, come in."

"Here, Lise. Where are you?" asked Denise.

"Over on Clarence Street at the Koper residence. One of our volunteers hazed a young cub down this street. Do you have any calls outstanding?"

"Just that one sighting. Steve and Braden are out looking for the mom."

Rory knew he was in her personal space, but she hadn't moved to get away from him, either. He stared into her eyes at the indigo blue surrounding her irises. Her lips parted, and she bit her bottom lip as she stared back at him.

Holding his gaze, she said, "Dispatch, I'm going to be out with Rory Gallagher. Tell Steve we're also looking for the mother."

"10-4, Lise," said Denise. "Be safe out there."

Be safe. Right now, he'd feel safer fifteen feet away from an angry polar bear mother than he did standing a hair's breadth from Lise Dumont. He opened the wooden door as she replaced her mic.

"After you." He managed not to let his voice crack. They headed out into the frosty air, Lise ahead of him. Pitch dark had descended on the town. The entire night rolled out ahead of them.

CHAPTER 3

Lise fastened her shotgun to the gun rack in the back of his truck and moved her supplies to the back seat. Large groups of children and adults walked door to door down the street while another truck drove past slowly. She waved back at the driver as he went by.

"We should go between the school and the ballpark area. The mother bear might have broken off and be hiding over that way," she said as she climbed in the front seat.

Rory turned over the engine and cranked up the heat. "Wherever you think is best. The school's a good idea." He pulled out and drove north and then turned left towards the elementary school. "We should drive around the outside and the ballpark."

"Dispatch, come in." She keyed her mic again.

"Go ahead, Lise," said Denise.

"Any more word about sightings of the mother bear?"

"No more calls. Steve has driven around the Town Centre and is going along the shore."

"10-4. We're heading over to the school and will drive past the church and Legion," said Lise.

She sank back into the contoured seat. His truck was

tricked out with every luxury option available. Naturally. He was a confirmed bachelor and could spend his money however he pleased. Why did that tick her off? She had a good-paying job. Well, now that she was back here, she did.

Men. Men and their power. Men and their money. Her mood wasn't improving, even though that was hardly his fault. She thought about those luxurious flowers he'd sent her and felt ashamed of herself. For about five seconds.

Their conversational lag was becoming awkward. Why didn't he speak? Was he waiting for her to mention the flowers? Of course, she should thank him. She turned towards him and opened her mouth.

"What are the odds that two people who are two percent of the entire world's population would wind up in the same town?" asked Rory.

"What?" Her mouth was still open.

"Us." He looked over at her and smiled as they rode over a huge ice ridge in the road. "We both have the kind of red hair that women pay big bucks to get in a salon."

"I'm not following you."

"Redheads. We make up two percent of the world's population," he said patiently as if she was one of the little girls trick-or-treating. "And you, having those incredible blue eyes, are even more of a rarity. Red hair and blue eyes are the rarest genetic combination of all. You make up 0.17 percent."

Flustered, she realized she hadn't put her seat belt on when they left, and she pitched into him as they went over another rocky patch on the road.

"Oomph!" She pulled away from him but didn't miss his smirk. It was the same smirk he had when his helicopter rotors had tangled up her hair on the beach. "Is that your idea of a pickup line?"

"No." He laughed, a deep, rich laugh with an edge of

nerves. "Although if I ever see another redhead up here, I could try it out, I suppose."

They'd arrived at the school, and she hadn't even noticed. Thoughts of looking out for a polar bear in the shadows hadn't even crossed her mind. She needed to get a grip on herself.

"I've never heard that statistic before." She sat back against the passenger door. "My parents are both redheads. Dad came here from Ireland when he was three, and my mother is French-Canadian. My sister is the same. It was normal in our family."

Rory put his high beams on and shone them towards the school, backing into a parking spot across from the ballpark diamond. Both the schoolyard and the park were surrounded by an eight-foot-high fence. Still, the alleys between nearby buildings were filled with snow drifts where a bear could hide. Lise had once tracked a polar bear from one end of town through these same alleys to the church at the other edge of town.

"Do you want me to drive right around the building? I don't see any tracks, but we can go slow and take a look," said Rory.

"Yes, please," she said, because right now, she just wanted to listen to his deep voice.

He put the truck in gear and drove towards the left side of the school while she took her flashlight and shone it out the passenger window down onto the snow. They bounced around the snow drifts and headed between the school and Grace Community Church.

"No tracks so far. I doubt she would've gone this far away from her cub."

"I'm surprised they got past your bait traps around the perimeter. Most of them fall for it," he said as he manoeuvred the truck around the corner. "She must be a first-time mom."

They came around the back of the school and church and

drove back and forth in the snowed-in parking lots. Both buildings were lit up like Canada Day fireworks, to help show up any bears who were wandering around town. Lise saw nothing that looked remotely like a bear.

"Where did your red hair come from then?" she asked. "Joy and your mom have such beautiful dark brown hair and eyes."

Instant chill in the truck cabin. She regretted the words as soon as she'd said them. Why did she mention their Indigenous looks? She could've slapped herself in the face. *Idiot*.

"Actually," he drew out the word, looking straight ahead as he pulled the truck out onto the road again, "I'm adopted." He kept driving, his fingers drumming on the steering wheel. "I would've thought that was pretty obvious."

Lise shook her head and let out a shocked sound, which she turned into a coughing fit. "Not to me, but mind you, if you ask Aid—" She stopped dead.

"Ask who?"

"Nothing. I was going to say, families are complicated, and red hair is a recessive gene, so you could've easily been a generation or two removed, you know?"

Now, he turned to look at her, a genuine smile on his face. "So, you think I'm the result of a liaison with a local Indigenous woman when the coureur de bois were going through here two hundred years ago?" He'd relaxed, so Lise's stomach unclenched. Even if she was upset with one man, she had no reason to insult this one.

"I have no idea of your family history; I just meant..." She was babbling. Babbling. "Oh, man, I'm so sorry!"

He laughed again, and the timbre of his voice warmed her through and through. She couldn't remember the last time she'd heard Aidan laugh.

"It's okay. I'm adopted. I'll tell you the story, but not tonight." He grinned. "It's a good story."

"Tell me! How old were you?"

"Practically a newborn. A few days old." His eyes flashed in the dashboard lights. "Seriously, I'll tell you but sometime when the time is right."

"Lise, come in." Denise's voice filled the truck.

She grabbed her mic and keyed it. "Lise here."

"Meet Ben at the detachment. He wants to see you guys with some volunteers."

"10-4. We're on our way."

Rory did a U-turn on the road. "Wonder if they need you for the bear." He gunned the truck down Kelsey Boulevard and out to the detachment. Trucks were lined up outside and parked with their back ends up to the sidewalk for a quick drive out.

Men and women packed the bullpen as they entered. Voices swirled around them as Rory put his hand to the small of her back to push her through the crowd. Ben was at the head of the room.

"Everyone, please. Your attention, please." Ben raised his left hand. His right hand rested on his utility belt and holster. The hubbub died down to a murmur, and Ben put both hands on his hips. "I called you all in because I don't want this going out on the radio. The Thompson RCMP notified us they had a jailbreak today, and there are two convicts at large."

Lise heard a woman gasp. Rory still had his hand on her back, and she wondered whether she should move sideways, or if it would make things more awkward. She was in uniform and didn't want to look like she needed a man holding on to her. She shifted to the left and put her weight on her left foot. Rory took back his hand like it was on fire. *Yep, awkward.*

"We searched the VIA Rail train that came in at eight tonight." Voices clamored around her. Two escaped convicts.

Great. As a peace officer, she'd be pulled into any search for them. Not that she was afraid of a manhunt.

"And," Ben continued, "we have no real reason to believe they're going to come this far north. One of them has family in Winnipeg, so they're likely heading there. I want everyone to be on the lookout for strangers—and I know this is polar bear season and the hotels are packed, but watch out for men who look like they don't belong in a tour group."

"Are they armed?" asked a bald man in the room's front. "The only way they're going to get up here is by train. No airline will let them board."

"That's a good point, Carl," said Ben. "That's why we're going to be at the train for every arrival. We have no reports of problems on any flights, but I wanted to let you bear volunteers know what's going on."

"What about them being armed?" A shrill female voice spoke up. "Did they hurt anyone in their escape?"

"I don't have full details yet," said Ben, "but I'm getting lists of all the guests from each of the hotels, so I have a headcount of how many male tourists we've got in town. And we're all armed because of where we live. I don't want anyone taking any potshots at a strange man because you're flinching." He stared hard at the group. "I mean it. No one, and I mean *no one*, is to be doing any shooting unless your life is directly threatened."

The group quieted down until all Lise could hear was raspy breathing and shuffling feet. Adrenaline sang along her veins. Just the thought of a manhunt made her stand taller. How could she ever have thought she could give up this job forever?

"All I have for descriptions are the photos Trudy's handing out to you now. They're not great photos, but they'll have to do. So, keep this off the radios and amongst yourselves. We probably won't see them, but we need to be ready if we do." Ben nodded at Lise and Rory in the rear. "Okay, if these escapees make it this far north, call it in, but it's up to the RCMP to apprehend them. Am I clear?"

"Yes, Ben, yes, Ben," the crowd responded. People folded the black and white paper photos and put their parkas back on. Rory took a picture and passed it to Lise. She stared down at the two brutal-looking men. One appeared to be in his late 20s, with piercing blue eyes. Darren Catcheway. The other was older, with a boxer's nose and balding head. His name was Karl Falhgren.

Both were doing significant time for murder. What was their plan, and how did they escape? She let people exit around her and folded the paper neatly in four squares, then put it in her left pocket.

"Time to get back on the road?" she asked Rory.

She spun around and was unnerved by how she could look straight into his eyes. She was tall, and Aidan had hated that about her. He'd taken to wearing shoes with lifts so he could stay two inches taller than her.

Rory quirked an eyebrow and nodded towards the front door. "Lead the way, ma'am. I'm at your service." His smile. That smile was a killer. And she still hadn't thanked him for the flowers. She headed towards the door, telling herself she'd do it in the truck and avoid any other conversational minefields while she was at it.

They had polar bears and escaped convicts to look for... that was enough excitement for one night.

Four hours later, Rory sat in his blue 4x4 pickup outside the Legion, his stomach crawling with need. He wanted a beer but realized that urge was because he was lonely. Drinking alone made him pathetic. He crossed his arms and leaned against the inside of the truck's door.

He'd dropped Lise off at the one apartment building in town over an hour ago. His truck seemed empty since they'd spent almost eight hours working together. The memory of her presence bloomed into the empty space in his cabin.

He watched groups of construction workers enter the brightly lit Legion, the doors swinging open and shut, mocking him with their teasing invitation to oblivion. Music filtered out into the frosty air and then died off as the door shut with a bang.

Waves of red-hot anger rippled through his veins. He pounded the steering wheel and gave it one huge whack with his right fist.

"Argh," he shouted in the confines of the cab of his truck.

Luckily, no one was in the parking lot to see his tantrum. He should back up right now and leave. Sweat bloomed down his spine and on his chest. If he still believed in God, he might've stood a chance against temptation. His belief in God had died the same day his father died in the Churchill River seven years ago.

The Legion door crashed open, and blaring music heralded a man and woman struggling together. The man yelled unintelligible words as the woman put a wrist lock on him and shoved him up against the door.

Rory jumped out of his truck and slammed the door, which made both crane their heads around to look his way.

"What's going on?" His voice was gravel.

The woman let go and stood back, panting. She flipped back her near waist-length hair and put her hands on her hips. Rory couldn't help but notice she'd pinned the guy fine against the door at the same time he realized it was Lise.

"Mind your own business," whined the drunk forty-something man. "It's a personal matter."

"Looks like a public matter to me," said Rory as he walked up to them.

"It's fine." Lise gathered up her flaming red hair and fastened it into a ponytail. "A misunderstanding about my character." She turned to face Rory. Arched red brows framed her blue eyes. Her firm pink lips shone with gloss. "He's not going to give me any more trouble, are you?"

The man swore under his breath and pushed past them to go back inside. Lise stepped back to let the door shut. She wore a navy blue turtleneck sweater, although Rory could tell it was expensive, not something bought over at Ruby's Emporium. And her jeans and leather belt were designer labels. Growing up with his sister Joy and about eight foster sisters, Rory had learned a lot about female fashion over the years.

"You're shivering; d'you want me to go get your parka? What are you doing here? I dropped you off at home," he said.

"You did, I just couldn't sleep." She tossed her ponytail over her shoulder.

"Ready to head back in?"

"Give it a minute." She crossed her arms over her ample bosom. "His buddies might decide to avenge him." She shot Rory a hard look. "I don't need anyone defending me."

He put up his hands in a sign of mock surrender. "No, ma'am. You were doing fine on your own. Apologies." He turned to go.

"What are you doing here?"

He looked back over his shoulder. He cocked an eyebrow and walked back over to her. He put his left hand on the wall beside her head, where she leaned against the wall, her breath pluming frost into the air.

"I guess all that searching for phantom escaped convicts

revved me up. Thought I'd take a drive down the shore, but I was still wound up. Thought I'd have a nightcap before I headed home."

She didn't flinch or move away from him. "Guess we had the same idea."

He flicked a lock of hair out of her face. "I haven't seen you in town for months. Were you on leave or something?"

"I've been away for a bit, and now I'm back." Something shadowed across her eyes. She bit her lip and straightened away from the wall. "I need a fresh drink. Heaven only knows what drugs that idiot put in my last one." She turned and wrenched open the door. "Join me?"

Rory stood, his hands shoved into the front pockets of his parka. He took in the tendrils of fiery red hair framing her pale face. Well, he wouldn't be drinking alone. "One drink, I guess."

She smiled. "I heard you were a teetotaler. C'mon, then."

They entered the Legion Hall, tables shunted together with bodies packed in shoulder to shoulder. She pulled him along by his right arm to the bar, where men parted like the Red Sea to make way for her. He recognized an 80s rock ballad blaring over the sound system. The air seemed to vibrate. Men stared covertly at her. Some stared openly. Those men he shut down with a hard glance.

Lise leaned over the bar and called for another beer, her gold earrings flashing in the LED lights around the mirrored bar. "What do you want to drink?"

Rory stood sideways to her. "I'm fine with a pop." He turned to the bartender. "I'll have a ginger ale, please." What was she up to? That shadow behind her eyes had grown. Her booted foot tapped frenetically to the beat on the floor. She gulped down a quarter of her beer, then slammed the bottle down on the bar.

"Do you want to find a seat?" he asked, curious why she was here alone. "Did you come with a girlfriend or someone?"

"Nope." She turned and rested her elbows on the bar. "Just had to get out of my apartment. I've been away, and it's so small... it was closing in on me. You know how it is."

Rory knew. Before he could put a sentence together, she'd polished off another half of the beer.

"Maybe you want to slow down there?" he said.

"Nope."

"Thanks," he said to the bartender, who handed him a bottle of ginger ale. "Why don't I drive you home?" He took a swig from the bottle.

Lise leaned into his personal space, her blue eyes rimmed with a deeper blue around the outside of the irises. "I wouldn't have invited you in here if I'd thought you were going to tell me what to do."

"And what is it you want to do?"

She wavered a bit and forced herself to lean against the bar. "Forget. Forget why I'm back here in this place and forget the past year and a half. Forget it all." She picked up the beer bottle and waved it back and forth. "Forget Aidan Grant." She tilted the bottle and drained it.

He grabbed her under the arms as her elbow missed the bar, and she sagged towards him. "Okay, I think that's it for you." He took the bottle away from her and shoved it towards the bartender. "Consider her cut off."

"I'm fine," she said, her face buried against his parka. At least, that's what he thought she said. She was still talking into his parka. "I can't hold my booze."

"Where's her coat?" He had to raise his voice at the bartender, who pointed towards the side of the door where there was a coat check. Great. Now, he had to manoeuvre her shaky legs over to it and then out the door.

He hooked her right arm around his neck and shoulder and put his left arm around her waist. She hadn't appeared drunk outside, but that last beer hit her like a polar bear diving for a seal. He brought them over to the coat check without too much trouble. She sang along to the music at full volume.

"Okay, my singing diva, let's get you dressed for the great outdoors."

The girl behind the counter took one look at them and brought out a hunter-green goose-down parka with a white woolen toque and scarf. He got her arms into the parka as she leaned on his shoulder.

"Can you hold on to something so I can zip you up?"

Her eyes sparkled as she kept singing along to the music, but she held still while he zipped her up and shoved the toque over her head. She grabbed the scarf and put it around her neck with a flourish.

"Ready, Freddy," she slurred.

He guided her the same way out to the front of the building. The door swung shut on the blast of music and voices. She put her left hand into his parka pocket as they walked out to the parking lot.

"I think that last beer was your one too many," Rory said. "And who's Aidan Grant, if you don't mind me asking?"

Lise leaned forward and threw up over her boots and snow. Rory grabbed her to keep her upright, then held her long ponytail back out of the way. He had to turn and look away, holding his breath. The last thing he'd ever admit was that he had a weak stomach and would throw up just because someone else did as well.

Finally, she finished getting rid of all the beer. Fat tears rolled down her cheeks, and her nose ran. Rory pulled her away from the mess and onward to his truck. He held her to one side while he opened his passenger door. He fished around in the console for some tissues. Tenderly, he wiped her face and mouth as she moaned.

"You're okay," he said. "Let's get in, and then you can relax." He lifted her into the passenger side and put her feet in. He ran around to the driver's side, got in, and fastened her seat belt. Her head fell back against the headrest, and a tear slid down the left side of her cheek.

She passed out.

Rory had no idea where her purse was, or which one was her vehicle. He looked over at her pale, beautiful face in the glow of the parking lot's light standard. Now, he remembered part of what Joy had said. Lise left Churchill to be married down south. She wasn't supposed to come back here. Obviously, something major had gone wrong for her to be back here and to want to forget the last year and a half.

One thing he never did was involve himself in other people's lives. Not his employees, his family, or his acquaintances around town. This wasn't his problem, but he knew where he could take her to sleep this off.

He started up the truck and drove out of the Legion parking lot. He could drop Lise off at Joy and Ben's place. Joy would take care of her, and Ben would help her get her vehicle in the morning. Problem solved. He rolled his tensed-up shoulders as he headed up Kelsey Boulevard to his sister's place. Lise was now Joy's problem.

CHAPTER 4

Lise heard humming. Incessant humming. And felt leatherette stuck to her cheek, but her head hurt too much to open her eyes. Maybe if she stayed curled up in this tight ball, the humming would stop, and she could go back to the oblivion of precious sleep.

"Emberlyn," Joy called, "get away from her and find your boots. The Sunday School bus is coming."

Mercifully, the humming stopped. Lise kept her eyes shut, but the warmth of the child's body stuck to her as Emberlyn leaned forward into Lise's personal space. She could smell peanut butter and toast on Emberlyn's breath. Lise scrunched her eyes tighter.

"Emberlyn, I'm not telling you again," Joy whispered from the living room door. "Get in here right now."

"But Mommy, I want to ask her about the polar bear," whispered Emberlyn, her sticky breath fanning over Lise's face.

"She's sleeping, and you need to get ready for the bus." Joy took her daughter by the hand and walked her out of the room. Lise could hear Emberlyn's plaintive whine fade into the kitchen. She wished she were still sleeping. What was she doing on Joy and Ben Koper's couch?

Lise pulled her right cheek away from the leatherette of the couch and pried open her crusted-over eyes. The sunlight coming in the front window hurt them, and she pulled the pillow up from the floor where it'd fallen and hefted it over her face to shut out the light. She had no memory of how she'd gotten here.

Her whole body ached. She crossed her arms over the pillow and wished for death. Broken images flitted through her mind. Men and music. People's bodies crushing against her, and the tang of cold beer against her tongue. She never drank beer; her one foray into drinking alcohol was the crisp fruitiness of a white wine at a cousin's wedding. The Legion didn't cater to such fine palates.

Oh, my word, I'm going to be sick...

With an instinctive rush, she hauled herself off the couch and ran into the kitchen, her hand over her mouth.

"Bathroom?" she gasped at Joy, who was washing the breakfast dishes.

"Upstairs at the top." Joy turned and pointed with her right hand.

Lise sprinted up the short flight of stairs, barely making it in time to heave up the meager remnants of her stomach's contents. She collapsed against the bathroom wall, tears falling as she flushed the toilet. She blew her nose with toilet paper and then sat and cried.

Joy appeared in the doorway and then perched on the edge of the tub. "Any better?" she said.

Lise shook her head. "I'm so sorry..." She sniffled and scrubbed her face with her hands, making her freckles stand out on her white skin. Her hair tangled around her shoulders, and she could smell her own stale sweat from her favourite cashmere sweater.

"You'll be okay," said Joy. "You need to rehydrate and take a couple acetaminophen."

"I don't remember calling you or coming here."

"Rory brought you over." Joy leaned forward with her elbows on her thighs, smiling.

"Rory? Your brother?" Lise covered her eyes with the heels of her hands. "Oh, my word, I can never face him again. I never even thanked him for the flowers, and now he's seen me like this..." She moaned.

"Hey, hey, it's going to be all right." Joy grabbed some tissues from the sink vanity. "Rory's discreet. That's why he brought you here. He didn't want you to be alone."

"I thought I was getting away from everything, but I've just made a huge mess of it, and how can I...?" She put her head down on her folded arms over her bent knees and cried.

"I will agree with you that drinking, or even going to the Legion, alone like that were bad ideas," said Joy. "But you can get past this, and Rory's not one to make judgments when he doesn't have all the facts."

Lise's head throbbed like a nail gun was piercing her eyes. At least her stomach felt better.

"What you need is some water and one of the sports drinks that I keep in the fridge for Emberlyn. You need to restore your electrolytes, and that'll help you feel better. And that acetaminophen and a shower." Joy stood, ever practical. "I say we start with the drink and painkiller first, then the shower."

Lise gulped in some deep breaths and blew her nose again. "I'm such an idiot. I'm never drinking again. I can't believe I let myself lose control like that, and in front of someone I..."

"In front of someone you...?" asked Joy, quirking up her left eyebrow with a smile.

"Someone I respect," Lise finished. "This will never happen again; I can promise you that much."

"Promise yourself, that's who counts," said Joy. "Okay, come on downstairs, and let's get you hydrated. Why don't I whip over to your place and get you a change of clothes?"

Lise followed Joy down the stairs to the kitchen. "I couldn't ask you to do that, and besides, what time is it?"

"Going on nine o'clock," said Joy.

"Oh, good grief, I should be at work! No, wait. It's Sunday."

"Nothing doing until you follow Nurse Joy's orders. Otherwise, you're going to be sick for the rest of the day." Joy rooted around in the fridge and brought out a bottle of red sports drink. "I want you to drink eight ounces of water and then all of this and take two of these painkillers before you do anything else."

"Do you have any crackers?" asked Lise.

Joy grinned. "Crackers coming right up. And I'm assuming you don't mean animal crackers?" She put some salted crackers on a plate and poured the sports drink into a tall glass. "I think things are likely pretty quiet since last night. I know the police scanner has been dead."

"Dead," groaned Lise. "That's exactly how I feel. Serves me right." She drank the offered glass of water and then drank a quarter of the sports drink. "Hmmm, weird taste, but not bad."

"I keep them for Emberlyn for when she brings home a gastro bug from school. Her grade two classroom is a petri dish for all kinds of viruses and bacteria."

"Listen, I can walk home on my own steam."

Joy pulled her into a hug. "In bear season? You really are hungover. I'll drive you over to pick up your car at the Legion."

The Legion. More images of last night flashed through her mind. Rory coming up to her and that stupid guy who'd grabbed her in the bar. She'd made quick work of him, but Rory had come back into the bar with her. She slammed her hand over her mouth.

"I threw up in front of Rory!" Tears filled her eyes again. "What if I have to work with him again?" Lise hung her head over the plate, wiping her eyes. "I'm such an idiot."

"Hey, let's not be too hard on ourselves, shall we?" Joy sat down opposite her and patted her shoulder. "We all make mistakes, and believe me, I've made bigger ones than you did last night."

"Did you almost marry a guy so fake you didn't even know him?" Lise swiped at her nose. "No, you didn't. You and Kira both married fantastic guys. I'm the one who can't tell a loser from a—I don't know what." She pressed her hands to her temples. "My head is pounding like a jackhammer."

Joy held out two white pills. "Take these. Nurse's orders. And maybe it's none of my business, but you've come back up here minus that enormous engagement ring you were sporting last spring. Kira would've been at the wedding, but bear season is their prime tourist time."

Lise palmed the pills and swallowed them with a hearty gulp of sports drink. "I've been stupid for a long time."

"Stop saying that! You're a solid peace officer, and you've fit in great up here. What on earth are you talking about?"

"I don't know..." Lise pushed back her mess of tangled hair. "I got carried away by all the attention Aidan foisted on me when he arrived up here last year. He found out every little thing I liked, whether it was food, or music, or where I wanted to travel someday." She took another swig of the sports drink. "When he went back down south, he texted me at all hours of the day and night, and I'd never had a guy do that before."

"And he was rich," said Joy.

"And he was rich," said Lise, "which I told myself wasn't such a big deal, but when he'd insist on paying for my flights down south to go see him, or when he started sending up his private plane just so I could go spend my turnaround shift with him, it really went to my head."

She picked the label off the sports drink bottle, flicking bits of the paper to the side of her plate. "I loved the attention from the pilot and the flight attendant. I mean, who wouldn't? It was like I was so special, to be his guest, and have him spend that kind of money on me... I just..."

"Who wouldn't feel special?" Joy smiled. "I know I would. I'd love it. Why are you so down on yourself?"

"Because I missed the red flags. Or, if I saw them, I told myself they didn't matter."

"I missed the red flags with Emberlyn's dad, too." Joy gave her a knowing look. "He was always on the run, working in the clinic supervising the resident doctors. Our, ah, relationship was definitely not his top priority." She wiped the table in front of them with a damp cloth. "What kind of red flags?" asked Joy.

Lise stared across the room, her chin in her hand. "It was minor stuff at first. I told myself I was nuts for even worrying about it. Aidan was always moving so fast, so busy all the time with his cell phone attached to his wrist because of his businesses. I told myself that's why he was doing it..." A single tear overflowed her right eye, and she swept it away.

"Doing what, hon?" said Joy.

Lise swiped at her tears and sniffled. "He'd do things like order my meals for me if we were eating out. No big deal, right? Except, he'd never ask me what I wanted to eat. He'd say, 'she'll have the fresh salad and trout, no rice. She doesn't need the carbs.' Stuff like that, or he'd order clothes for me and have them waiting for me when I arrived at his place."

Joy got up and picked up a box of tissues from the kitchen counter. She brought the crackers over to the table and pushed the tissues in front of Lise, who sat with tears rolling down her face.

"The clothes were more expensive than anything I'd ever been able to afford in my life. Silks and cashmere, and designer dresses, but I never went shopping for them. He decided what he wanted me to wear. It started after I'd brought down a dress for some business dinner he wanted to take me to, and he said he didn't like me in purple. He whipped out this red dress from a closet and didn't explain *why* he had a woman's dress on hand and told me that was what I was wearing for dinner."

Joy's eyebrows rose. "So, it was more of an order to wear it than a request."

"Yes, and after that, every time I went to visit on my days off or we went on vacation, he had clothes bought and ready for me. He expected me to take them home with me. At first, I told myself he was being generous, but at the back of my mind, I kept thinking, he doesn't think I'm good enough the way I am."

"Umm hmm," Joy murmured.

"At first, he pretended to be impressed with my job, but eventually, he admitted he hated it. Why should I be worried about conservation and saving polar bears? Why would I want to be close to such dangerous animals?"

"What did he want you to do?"

Lise blew her nose daintily. "He wanted me to quit and not work. When he proposed to me, down in St. Maarten's, he made it clear that now I could stop working and just enjoy life and 'keep house' for him. And because he owned four houses, he said that would keep me busy enough."

"Wow, I don't even know what to say to that," said Joy. "He thought you'd be happy being some kind of trophy wife, hanging around the house all day while he worked at whatever the business of the day was, and you'd do basically nothing?"

"Exactly," said Lise. "That's what his mom does, and his sister, who's married to some guy who's worth even more than Aidan is, so naturally, he wasn't going to have me working." She took a deep breath. "And he wanted me to move all of my money over so he could 'invest' it for me. I told him I already had investments."

"I see," said Joy. "I need another coffee. How're you doing for fluids there?" She got up and poured herself a cup of coffee and then pointed to Lise's bottle of sports drink.

"I'm good, thanks." Lise swirled around the last bit of red sports drink in the bottle. "His mom didn't really care for me, but I could've dealt with that," she said.

"Oh, don't count on it," said Joy. "If they don't like you beforehand, they rarely change their minds."

"Well, she'll be hating me for sure now."

"Why? What did you do?" asked Joy.

"I walked out on him two weeks before the wedding," said Lise.

Joy choked on her coffee. She grabbed a tissue to wipe up what she'd coughed all over the table.

"He and I got into a big fight at home one night. He found out I didn't actually resign from my job up here." Lise paused and wiped her eyes again. "He demanded that I do it, and I refused. I said I needed time to think about it. He shoved his finger in my face. Told me I had no other option but to marry him. I had nowhere else to live, he said, so where did I think I could go? When he stormed off, I took off out the front door of our condo and left."

"He actually said that to you?" said Joy. "That's insane. You know all of that behaviour was abusive, right?"

Lise's eyes filled with tears. "If they give you a black eye, people believe you. I realized I couldn't go through with the wedding. I needed to escape."

"Oh, Lise! I'm so glad you did and that you came back up here to your friends." Joy took Lise's two hands in hers and squeezed them. "I believe you. There's no way a man who loves you treats you like that—you did the right thing."

"I am done with him." Lise bowed her head. "He's texted me a gazillion times. He's just about blown up my phone. Look here." She pulled her hand away and took her cell phone out of her jeans pocket, handing it over to Joy.

Joy scrolled through the belligerent texts. "Lise, do you think he's going to come up here after you? You should talk to Ben."

"No, he's a big talker, but I don't see him flying up here. You can see in this text..." She took the phone from Joy. "Here– *I told our friends I'd called off the wedding because I'd found photos on social media of you with another guy. I hope you rot in hell. Return that ring if you know what's good for you.*"

"Oh my, Lise! He sounds almost dangerous."

"He might be, I don't know." She put the phone down on the table. "And I'm sorry my parents had to deal with that announcement, but my mother's busy texting me, telling me to make up with him! She's desperate for me to marry into his rich family if you can believe it."

"What are you going to do about the ring?"

Lise snorted and coughed on her sports drink. "I drove straight to a courier service, insured it for half a million dollars, and sent it right back to him. I know they delivered it before he sent that text, and I have proof. He's blowing off steam."

Joy scrolled down on the mobile phone, reading more of the texts. "Still, maybe you should seek some legal advice?"

"I want to forget I ever made such a stupid mistake."

"Well, there's a new lawyer in town if you change your mind. Matt Jaeger." She handed Lise her phone back.

"Thanks. I'll see how it goes. I don't care about the wedding gifts; he can send them all back. I'm waiting for my mother to calm down." Lise took another sip of her sports drink. "She's far more likely to show up here than he will."

"Don't you think your mother will want you to be happy?" said Joy.

Lise huffed and shook her head. "My mother wanted me to quit this job and be a society lady. Bring some pizzazz to the family. She never could understand why I love this job so much, so they were the perfect pair."

"I'm sorry. It's tough when your parents don't get you." Joy swirled the remains of her coffee around in her cup.

Lise sat back in her chair and sighed. "I had a boyfriend in high school she adored. He was a complete jerk. Now *he* left marks on me all the time."

"Lise!" Joy's shock was palpable. "Didn't your parents do anything about it?"

"He'd hurt me or punch me with his fist where you couldn't see it. On my upper arms or thighs, where my clothes covered me. I had enormous bruises all the time."

"And why did your mother think this guy was so great?"

Lise flipped her hair back again and shrugged. "He was a sicko. He'd flirt with her, and she seemed to like the attention. I admit—" she stared off into space, "he was the best-looking guy I'd ever dated or even seen. We considered him a real catch. But whenever he'd pinch me or punch me, he'd tell me to suck it up or grow up. Like I wasn't tough enough."

"Oh, Lise, that's awful." Joy reached across the table and squeezed her hand. "How did it end?"

"Luckily for me, he was a year ahead of me and graduated. He went away to college because his parents insisted." Lise's stomach rolled over as she spoke about him. "Who knows what he did to his next girlfriend?"

"I'd say you got off that roller coaster just in time," said Joy.

"I felt the same fear when Aidan shoved his finger in my

face. The rage in his eyes—I can't even describe it. I needed to get away from him."

"I'm so sorry you went through that, but you made the right decision."

"I know." Lise smiled faintly. "I have such bad luck with men. Or maybe I just pick the wrong ones."

"Nothing wrong with taking a break," said Joy. "Let's go get your car, and you can get some rest at home."

Lise stood and took the sports drink bottle over to the blue recycling box. She pulled the neckline of her cashmere sweater to her nose and pretended to cross her eyes at Joy.

"This reeks of smoke and, ugh... me. We don't have a dry cleaner up here, either. Aidan gave it to me, so I'll probably throw it out." She stood looking out the kitchen window at the snowy street. "I've taken up enough of your time."

Joy put her hand on the young woman's shoulder. "Hey, don't do that. That's what friends are for, right?"

Lise turned and smiled at her wanly. "Well, next time you go off the rails, be sure and call me." She went to the back door and started pulling on her high-end leather boots. "I can't believe Rory drove me all the way over here, and I don't remember a thing."

Joy flipped her truck keys in her hand. "Remember to take some more acetaminophen in six hours if the headache doesn't go away."

"Yes, Mom," said Lise. She smiled wanly again and pulled on her parka from the hook on the back door. She wanted to race home and shower off the effects of last night and wash them away forever. Along with all memories of Aidan. If only it were that easy.

She headed down the side stairs to the parked truck, the bright sunlight slicing into her red-rimmed eyes. She'd give anything for Rory not to have seen her in that state.

Could she have made any more of a fool of herself in front of him?

The frigid air outside hurt Rory's face as he entered the RCMP detachment carrying a couple of coffees from his mother's Café. He welcomed the flair of warmth from inside the bullpen.

"Anyone want a fresh brewed cup of joe?" he asked the room. He put the cardboard carrier down on top of Trudy's desk.

Adam's head popped out from around a computer screen. "I'll take one. Double double, please."

"Is Ben in yet?" asked Rory as he poured two creamers and two sugar packets into a large paper coffee cup and stirred.

"He's checking on the two guys we have back in holding. They're almost ready to be released."

"It was a nice quiet Halloween," remarked Rory as he carried Adam his coffee. His own coffee was in his right hand. "Other than that mother bear and her cub."

"Yeah, compared to last year, it was a breeze." Adam leaned back in his office chair. "Thanks for this, bud."

"Any more word on those two escapees?"

"No one's seen them," said Adam. "They must've had outside help because they've vanished into thin air, as they say." He took a sip of the steaming brew.

"How did they break out? I thought Thompson jail was medium security."

"I think it was on a court transfer. They overpowered the court officers and took off in their cruiser, which was recovered about an hour later." Adam pushed the mug sheets forward. "Did you get copies of these?"

"Yeah, last night," said Rory. "They're not likely to wind up here. Am I right?"

Adam shrugged. "Not likely. Maybe another car was waiting for them. Thompson RCMP are going through street camera footage now, and Winnipeg police contacted their families already. I guess they'll be staking out their family and friends."

"Hey, man, thanks for your help last night." Ben entered the bullpen and clapped Rory on the shoulder. "Another Halloween with no injuries to report. My kind of holiday."

"Who've you got back there?" asked Rory as he flicked his thumb towards the back cells.

"Ah, just a bar fight from The Great Northern Lodge. Couple of yahoos on a tour."

Rory laughed. "Jake's not used to that kind of goings on at his place."

"No, no, he's not. Is one of those for me?" asked Ben as he picked up a coffee cup and stripped off the plastic lid.

"The Lodge is trying to maintain a genteel atmosphere, especially since Kali McIntyre took over. I don't imagine she was too thrilled with her broken tables and chairs last night," said Adam.

"When are those two getting hitched, anyway?" asked Rory.

"Who knows?" Ben smiled. "This town could use another wedding. Why don't you put the bug in his ear?"

"I'm the last guy to suggest someone should get married," said Rory.

"Yeah?" said Adam, sipping more coffee. "You're more of the lone wolf type, are you?"

"Very lone, and very wolf." Rory raised an eyebrow. "Not that it's easy to find a woman who wants to live up here on the edge of *the wild nothingness,* as the person from my last fated relationship called it."

"That was back in high school," said Ben, trying to keep a solemn face.

"High school?" crowed Adam. "You haven't had a girlfriend since high school?"

"She was the daughter of the principal, and he got transferred *back to the real world,* as she called it," said Rory. "Broke my heart. Never again."

Ben clapped him on the shoulder again. "I sure hope you're kidding there, buddy. Emberlyn needs some cousins to play with."

"Why don't you and my sister give her a little brother or sister to play with?" asked Rory, grinning over the top of his coffee cup. "Leave me out of it, thanks."

The men started laughing just as Lise walked in. Her hair gleamed with red and gold highlights. She'd donned the classic Churchill garb: jeans, winter boots, and a long-sleeved T-shirt with a plaid flannel shirt over top. Rory couldn't help but notice that her curves were apparent through her open parka.

And once again, she had no hat on. The temperature was well below -25 Celsius out there. What was up with no headgear? Maybe she was vain about the riot of red hair curling all over her head and falling to her shoulders?

She stopped dead at the front counter at the sound of their laughter and rocked from one foot to the other, taking in who was sitting in the bullpen.

"I can come back, Ben," she stumbled.

"No, we're just... having a coffee, Lise. What can I do for you?" said Ben.

"I'm locked out, and I can't raise Braden. Is there any way you have a key for the community office?"

"Yeah, we've got a master key here somewhere. What's up?"

Rory inched closer to the empty desk near the counter. Despite himself, her electric presence drew him. Was she avoiding his eyes? He shifted sideways as he sat nonchalantly on the desk, his coffee cup resting on his right thigh. Yes, yes, she was definitely avoiding looking at him.

"George called me from the Polar Bear Jail. He said he's got a bear that's over the thirty-day limit, and he wants it moved up north as soon as we can. I wanted to check the bear reports myself in the office." She paused and cleared her throat. "Not that I don't believe him. We're full up there, but I wanted to check the last location we let one go."

She stepped back from the counter and huddled within her parka. Rory stopped trying to catch her eye and waited to see if she was going to ask what he hoped she would ask. He concentrated on drinking his lukewarm brew. Lise looked a bit peaked out of his peripheral vision.

Ben rustled around in a drawer on this side of the counter. "I think this is it." He handed it to her with a huge grin. "Glad to see you're no longer comatose."

Her face blushed crimson. "Gee, aren't you a—" She grabbed the key from Ben's outstretched fingers and turned to run out the door. "Thanks." She threw up her hood over her hair and raced out of the small foyer into the street.

"That was cruel," said Rory, depositing his empty coffee cup in the garbage pail beside the desk.

"What?" asked Adam.

"She knows I didn't mean anything by it," said Ben.

"Yeah, that's why she jack-rabbited it out of here and probably right into a bear's jaws." Rory pushed through the gap in the counter and tore through the two doors out into the street.

He did a quick double-take side to side for bears and saw Lise running around her blue car to the right.

"Lise!" he bellowed.

She yanked open the driver's door and jumped in the front seat. He raced over to the car and around the front end, rapping on the driver's window. Her face still fiery red, she lowered the window halfway.

"You shouldn't be outside," she bit off.

"Fine, let me in," he said, slightly out of breath at his sprint.

"Why?"

"Just let me in."

She hit the electronic locks, and he ran around the front end of the car again, jumping into the passenger seat and slamming the door. He rubbed his hands together from the freezing cold.

Lise leaned back until she touched her window. Inside the compact car, his knees were up to his chest. She sat and stared at him while the colour receded from her face. He considered his next words.

"My brother-in-law can be a bit of a jerk sometimes." He tapped his fingers on his left knee. "Or, a tease, depending on who's on the other end of his sense of humour."

"I thought your brother-in-law was the hero who could do no wrong." She folded her arms across her chest. That was a bad sign.

"He's definitely a hero, but his sense of humour isn't for everyone." Rory eased sideways in the small front seat. "I'm sorry. He shouldn't have said that to you."

"You don't have to apologize for him." Her intense blue eyes were slightly red-rimmed, but otherwise, he could smell lavender wafting from her hair. He appreciated her fondness for floral scents.

"No, but I was the one who took you over to his place, so I'm halfway responsible."

She turned away and played with her parka zipper. Silence filled the car, and he cast around for something to say, something brilliant or witty that would bridge the gap between sincerely feeling sorry for her and wanting to get to know her better. Nothing was coming to him.

Finally, she broke the silence. "Why did you take me over to Ben and Joy's house? Why didn't you take me to my place?"

"I didn't know where your purse was or which car was yours, so I—I improvised. Did you get your purse back, by the way?"

"Yeah, the janitor at the Legion gave it to me. Thanks." She stared out the front window. "I'm the one who should be saying sorry. I'm sorry you had to take care of me, and…"

"Hey," he interrupted, "no harm, no foul. We all get a little wild sometimes. I'm glad I was there, and that guy left you alone."

"He wasn't really a problem." She crossed her arms again. "And I'm sorry, I probably threw up on your boots." She turned to him, finally, and her eyes glistened with unshed tears. "I haven't been myself lately."

He lifted his hands off his knees in a conciliatory gesture. "You didn't barf on me, and no apology is necessary." He pretended not to notice the tears when what he really wanted to do was find a tissue and lean over and… what in the world was getting into him?

"Yeah, well, what are you going to do about this bear? Do you need a ride today?"

There. He'd said it. She obviously wasn't going to, and he needed to warm up the social temperature in the vehicle.

"A ride? We're in my car right now."

"I mean a helicopter. To take the bear up north." He

pressed his lips together to keep from grinning. She obviously was still fuzzy from her hangover.

"Are you sure your helicopter is safe to fly?" She straightened and put the key into her ignition. "I'm not interested in falling out of the sky."

"Touché. You wound me." He pretended to be stabbed in the chest. "I own three helicopters, although that one is being repaired." He gave her a head bob. "I'm at your service, milady."

"Fine," she said. "Let's fly that bear up to Arviat."

Her navy blue eyes still gleamed with unshed tears, but he loved her spunk. Today promised to be anything but boring.

CHAPTER 5

Where was he? Lise had tranquilized the polar bear and hooded its eyes. George stood in the open barn doors of the building, checking his mobile phone for the weather forecast. She was afraid they would be under the gun to get the bear up north before the tranquilizer medication wore off.

She'd dropped Rory off at his truck and arranged to meet him here at the Polar Bear Jail. He said he wanted to go home to feed his cat—*feed his cat?*—in case they were delayed and get warmer clothing on. She'd also gone back to her place and put on her winter uniform, which included her survival gear.

Now, she waited to hear the *whop-whop-whop* of his helicopter rotors coming down from the airport. She double-checked the bear's position in the netting on the wooden platform. Her headache was worse, but she'd grabbed a couple of pain pills at home.

George came back to her and showed her his phone screen. "I think you should cross over the Nunavut border and dump him off along the coast. There's no point in getting too close to Arviat. There's a storm front coming in from the northwest. Looks like we could get our first blizzard."

She peered at the red indicator on the map on his phone. "I

wasn't planning on going right near the town." She restrained herself from rolling her eyes. "I want this bear far enough away that he doesn't come back down here."

George nodded, his greying hair flopping over his forehead. He'd worked there so long he was an unofficial "boss" to the Conservation officers. "Leave him on the coast, and he'll be fine. The sea ice will be firmed up in a couple of days."

"If bad weather's coming, do we really need to do this today?" asked Lise.

"You'll be back before it hits. We're too full. I've got a mother and cub in the last stall."

The sound of the helicopter approaching could be heard down the highway. Ripples of nerves ran along her arms. She didn't enjoy flying at the best of times. Her stomach was still rocky, and she wished she was tucked in bed at home under her weighted blanket.

The ground snow blew up in clouds as the helicopter landed to the left of the building. She ran to the wooden trailer out front and picked up the hitch with George's help. They hauled the trailer around towards the helicopter as Rory turned off the rotors, and the chopper came to a standstill.

He jumped down with ease and came towards them. "Wait, I can help you."

She gave him a bit of room to join them but was determined to do her part. The three of them dragged the trailer closer, and then Rory ran back to the helicopter to get the hook and tackle from the bottom.

The men put the massive hook through the four metal circles of the net and ensured it was on straight. George stood by the bear and trailer as Rory and Lise headed back and got into the helicopter. Her stomach lurched again as she got into the seat and put on the three-point harness.

Rory flipped all the switches to fire the machine back up.

He put on his headset and passed one over to her. "This will help you hear me and anyone else we need to talk to on the way."

"Thanks." She put it on after scraping her curls back behind her ears. "We need to get this guy over the Nunavut border, and we can put him down along the coastline."

"No problem," said Rory.

He signaled to George, who gave him the thumbs-up sign beside the trailer. Rory pulled on the collective, and they gently rose into the air, the tackle leveling out below them and tightening as it got to the hook in the net around the bear.

"Okay, here we go," he said as they hoisted the bear off the wooden platform and into the air. "Nice and easy." He kept the helicopter even and steady, and Lise held onto her stomach, praying that her sports drink and crackers from the morning would stay down.

Lise leaned over to see if she could check on the bear but couldn't see him from her seat.

Rory looked at her with a huge grin. "Don't worry. I can tell by the drag he's still safely hanging." He tapped on the joystick. "We're only about five hundred feet up. How're you doing?"

She swallowed and kept her hand on her stomach. "Fine. As long as I don't think about the fact that I'm in a four-seater aircraft."

"Look out at the horizon line. That'll help your stomach," he said.

"How's your cat?" She couldn't think of anything intelligent to say, so she might as well find out about his cat.

"Bosco is fine. He got his favourite chow and a bit extra. Do you like cats?"

Her stomach was flipping over. She was in grave danger of hurling again from the weight of the wind buffeting the helicopter. Could she carry on a conversation and not throw up at the same time?

"I grew up with cats and dogs, but I haven't been settled long enough to have a pet of my own." She put her hand to her mouth. A bit of a lie. Aidan hated animals and had decreed a no-pet rule for their upcoming marriage.

Rory reached down to his right and then handed her a white reinforced paper bag. "This is one like the airlines use. It's a barf bag."

She couldn't hold back any longer. Despite her shame, she lost her drink and crackers. She knew from the heat of her skin that she was scarlet with embarrassment. Could this day get any worse?

"Just close the tabs and put it down beside your seat." He nodded towards the floor.

Mortified, she closed it and placed it beside her. That was twice now she'd upended her stomach in front of him. He must think she was a complete loser.

"People throw up in the air all the time," he said, as if reading her mind. "Especially little kids. It's rare not to have someone on a tour barf." He smiled at her. "No worries, okay?"

She pulled a tissue from her pocket and turned away as she wiped her mouth.

"Do you get airsick on planes too?" he asked.

Lise shook her head. "I get nauseous sometimes, but I don't actually, you know, do this..." She struggled to keep her eyes on the horizon. "Can I ask, why a cat? Why don't you have a humongous dog like every other guy up here?"

He laughed, and she decided it was a reassuring laugh. A laugh that made her feel safe.

"Dogs seem to be needy to me."

She looked at him in shock. "Needy?"

"Yeah, a dog follows you around everywhere you go. It

needs to be let outside, back inside; it needs exercise. Cats, they're independent. Bosco rarely gives me attention unless he's decided I've earned it." He laughed again, his eyes crinkling up at the sides. "I guess I'm too independent to want a dog on my heels all the time."

"I've never heard anyone say dogs are too needy." She laughed. "Most of the dogs up here are half wolf, half husky, and I wouldn't classify them as *needy*."

Rory shrugged. "You haven't lived up here all your life."

"That's true. I guess I have a way to go to lose the *city girl* stigma." She put quotation marks with her fingers around the words city girl.

"I don't see you as a city girl," he said. "I think you fit in up here just fine."

"Wow. That's a genuine compliment coming from you."

His baritone laugh filled the cockpit again. "How so?"

"All I know about you is that you're a confirmed bachelor who lives on the edge of the tundra, and you don't mix with the townsfolk that much." She arched an eyebrow at him. "In fact, I was shocked to see you having coffee with the cops this morning."

"You make it sound like I'm some fairy tale ogre living in the wilderness who hates the townspeople and lurks beside bridges for fair maidens to cross his path."

"Absolutely. A fairy tale ogre fits the bill." She laughed, feeling her stomach settle and watching the bluish snow and ice below them fly by. Stunted brown trees poked up from hillocks of frozen snow undulating across the tundra.

"My niece, Emberlyn, will love to hear that," he said.

"How much farther?" Lise turned to him and took in his strong profile.

His red stubble across his lower face was de rigueur for men up north. Not quite a beard, not quite clean shaven. His hair was shorter than most wore it, shaven on the sides with brushed-up curls on top. Her gaze went to his strong, square, freckled hands on the controls.

"About another five to eight minutes," he said, turning sideways to grin at her like some kind of Irish leprechaun. His eyes were such a light brown they were almost amber. She shook herself to get her wayward thoughts under control.

"Are you cold?" he asked. "There's no real heater in these things."

"I'm fine," she lied. Well, not cold anyway. She was way too warm with the way her body was overreacting to his nearness. "I'm concerned our guest is going to wake up early."

He nodded as he concentrated on the joystick as they flew. A few minutes went by with him humming under his breath.

"How long have you been a Conservation officer anyway?" he asked.

"Going on five years now. I did two years in Riding Mountain National Park in southern Manitoba, and when this posting came up, I jumped on it."

"How long is a posting? Is it like the RCMP?" he said.

"It depends on where it is and if you want to get into a supervisory role. I want to stay here if I can. I've applied for Steve Olds' job." She shaded her eyes against the snow glare. "I should hear in a couple of weeks. He's retiring."

"I hope you get it," he said. "Here, take my sunglasses." He passed over a pair. "How're your eyes doing?"

She accepted them gratefully. Her eyes were burning, and her head throbbed from the noise of the engine. Those pain pills hadn't kicked in yet.

"Thanks. Let's just say this is my first and will be my *only* hangover ever."

Rory laughed again, but it wasn't unkind. "I hear you. I'll do anything to avoid barfing myself. We had one little foster kid who used to eat dirt all the time and then throw it up. She kept my mom busy! My folks actually wanted to adopt her, but Children's Aid sent her back to her birth mother and stepfather."

"How awful! Why would a child do that?" Lise shuddered. "I can't imagine wanting to eat dirt."

"It's called pica. It's an eating disorder, and in her case, she'd been semi-starved from neglect."

"And Children's Aid sent her back to her family?" Lise couldn't keep the shock out of her voice.

Rory shrugged. "They worked with them to get better food security and a job for the stepdad. They didn't live in Churchill; they were further north. Mom worked wonders with that little girl, though."

"I love your mom. Everyone loves your mom." She could feel the heat in her cheeks again.

He gave her another grin. "You're right there. How does that look for setting this guy down?" He pointed towards the rocky shore coming up to the right. The wind blew strongly against them, and low purple clouds rushed alongside them to the left.

She peered out the front windshield. "Yeah, it's close to the slushy ice, and he might find some krill or something before the sea ice is hard enough." She nodded. "Let's do it. I'm worried he's going to wake up."

Rory slowed the helicopter to hover over a flatter section of the shore back from the actual water's edge. Still about four hundred feet in the air, he gently lowered the collective to bring the netted polar bear down to the ground. The tricky manoeuvre made Lise's stomach fall twice as the helicopter swayed back and forth.

Once the bear touched land, Rory fiddled with the joystick and flew the helicopter backwards. Lise realized she'd been holding her breath and blew it out slowly. The long tackle attached to the bear gave them some room between them and the bear. Rory turned off the engine and rotors.

"Let's check him out," Lise said as she opened the plexi-glass door and jumped down from the aircraft. "I want to make sure he's in a suitable position to wake up."

She hastened towards the bear and, with Rory's help, moved its front paws outwards from its sides. She removed the black hood from its eyes and checked its pupils, which were reactive. "Yeah, he's waking up all right."

They placed its head gently forward, too, upright on its chin. She took a few photos of it with her camera and of the surrounding landscape. The polar bear began lifting its head, moving to the left side.

"Okay, time to go!" Lise grabbed the black hood off the ground and sprinted towards the helicopter, Rory right behind her. They scrambled into the safety of the helicopter as they watched the bear roll its shoulders from side to side and gather its hind legs under it. The bear rose to its feet, unsteady but quite awake, and sniffed the frigid air.

"We did it!" Rory fist-pumped her. "Well done, Officer Dumont."

Snow fell sideways against the helicopter and wafted around the outside bubble of the cockpit. She could see the dark clouds pressing down on them now, almost as if they could touch them. The brilliance of the snow was stark against the bluish-purple of the clouds.

"It feels like we're in a snow globe," she said as Rory started up the engine and rotors again.

"That storm is going to blow us home," he said. They lifted off the ground and swung around towards the south. "We'd better make tracks."

"Think we'll beat it?"

"Oh yeah," he said, peering ahead through the dancing snowflakes. "I actually love flying in this kind of weather."

"I'd like to swing down south of town, in that case, and check out something."

"How far south?"

"Over towards the maternity dens on the border of Wapusk National Park," said Lise. "I heard there was some bear activity over that way. Do we have enough time to swing over and see if the females I'm thinking about are there?"

"Do you have coordinates or are you guesstimating?" said Rory.

"Not as far as the border of the park. Steve and Braden were patrolling out there last week, and I thought we could take a peek."

"We can give it a try," he said. "It's up to the weather, though."

She nodded her head and smiled. Her stomach was settled, and her headache was a dull throb. If they could get a glimpse of the female bears for a head count, she'd have a start on her report on the maternity dens.

Rory kept the helicopter level at about six hundred feet, and she felt stronger as they flew along the snowy wasteland. The tumbling clouds chased them from behind, and the harsh snow pelted the plexiglass canopy of the helicopter.

She could feel the tension in Rory's body beside her. "Are you sure you want to do this?" he asked her. "I don't want to get into an icing situation."

"We can turn back if you think it's too dangerous," she said. "I'm not the expert."

"I never back down from a challenge, but..." He grinned at her. "We're getting into some dicey wind up here."

"Okay, we can check it out another day," she said. "Hey, do you see that?" She pointed to the right.

Snow swirled around them now, obscuring part of their vision, but ahead, she could see a small red and white plane on its belly with a wing sitting up at an angle. It had skipped like a stone over the snow, and Lise could see the gouge marks where the plane had scattered rocks on its path of destruction. She couldn't see any propellers because the nose was blown open with wires sprawling against the snowdrift.

"Yeah, hang on." Rory swung around to get a better look through the wind-driven snow. "Can you see anyone?"

"No, I can't." Lise leaned forward, peering through the front of the canopy.

"Churchill, JR one," Rory radioed. They got static on the line.

"Is that a plane crash?" Lise wished the words back in her mouth the second she said it. Of course, it was a plane crash. They shouldn't see anything out here but snow, ice, and the odd wind-blown, stunted tree trunk.

"Churchill, JR one, come in," Rory said again. "I don't know why they're not hearing me."

He brought the helicopter in low and flew over the top of the plane. It looked like the type of four-seater plane used for sport hunting. The tail numbers were painted over, and the left wing had sheared off and lay crumpled to one side.

"Wouldn't we have heard about any planes crashing out here?" asked Lise.

"Not if their ELT device has been disabled," said Rory. "It might've been broken in the crash, or they might've forgotten to test it before they left. If there's no signal going to the satellites, then emergency services won't be notified that they're out here."

Lise leaned over as far as her seat belt would allow. "I don't see anyone down there. Should we go check?"

"Yeah, I want to do a quick check in case they're trapped inside. Hold on."

Rory put the helicopter down sideways to the crash site and turned off the rotors and engine. They both unhooked their seat harnesses just as the left skid shifted and spun sideways.

Rory muttered a curse under his breath as Lise gasped. He tore off his headset. Lise lurched downwards against the glass door on the left side of the aircraft.

"I've got you," he said as he finished undoing her harness and pulled her up towards himself.

"What happened?" She held onto the front of his parka as the helicopter shifted sideways again from the wind.

"There's more ice on top of this pack than I thought. Let's try and get out before anything else happens."

He swung open his own door and then jumped into the snow. Lise turned and came out backwards into his arms.

"Whew! What now?" she said as she turned back to face him. Their breath mingled together in the frosty air, and snowflakes swirled around their heads.

"We'll check out the plane for any passengers. Do you have a flashlight?" He gave a short laugh. "Should've asked you before we got out."

"We don't need a flashlight," said a gravel voice behind them. "We need you two to get back in there and get this bird in the air."

Lise gripped Rory's upper arms with a death grip. The business end of a shotgun filled his vision, along with a dirty man in mismatched clothes not fit for this kind of weather. Rory's whole body hardened as he turned his head to look at the intruder.

"Who're you?" he demanded.

"I'm the guy commandeering this helicopter. And you're the guy who's flying me and my partner the heck out of here."

CHAPTER 6

Rory took in the shotgun and the man's face from the poster at the same time. Lise let go of his parka and swung around towards the man in one smooth motion, pulling out her SIG Sauer P226.

"Stand down," she said, holding her gun two-handed and pointing it at the man's chest.

The blue-eyed convict gave a guttural laugh. "Guess what we've got here is one of them Mexican standoffs." Ice frosted his pale eyebrows, as well as his scrawny moustache. His arms remained rigid as he held the shotgun horizontally towards them.

"Lise," murmured Rory, "let's be careful here. Don't do anything rash."

"I'm a peace officer, and you're under arrest," she said, staring at the man whose skinny body shook inside a light jacket and pants that weren't meant for the outdoors and definitely not for the oncoming blizzard.

"Sure, honey bunch. I'm under arrest." He motioned forwards with the barrel of the shotgun. "Now, turn around and get back in. We're all going for a ride out of here."

"Where's your buddy?" Lise still held her gun poised, as

still as a statue, much to Rory's admiration. She'd snapped into officer mode, no longer worried about teasing conversation or last night's mistakes.

"He got hurt." The man bit his cracked bottom lip. Blood oozed from his nose and cuts on his forehead. "He's back there. Stuck." He tilted his head back towards the plane crash.

"How bad, Darren?" she asked.

"How do you know my name?" His shoulders went up around his ears, his stance more aggressive.

"Lise," said Rory again, a low warning in his tone.

"Everyone knows who you two are," she said, standing still. "Your buddy is Karl Fahlgren. You escaped from Thompson on a court detail. How bad is Karl hurt?"

Time telescoped inside Rory's vision and whirred by his head along with the wheeling snowflakes. He edged to the left of Lise so he could be useful if he needed to charge the man.

"We have a first aid kit," he said, bringing his hands out into the open and upward to his waist. "Why don't we try to help your friend?"

Darren's nose twitched. His gloved hands moved slightly on the shotgun. "First aid kit won't help him none."

"Let's see what we can do first, and then we can talk about getting out of here," said Rory.

"Put your gun away," said Darren to Lise. "I'll shoot your pal here." He waved the front end of the shotgun at Rory.

"Nobody's shooting anyone," Lise said, as if the guy was in cuffs instead of standing ten feet apart with death in between them.

Rory's knees weakened. He marveled at Lise's composure under fire. Willing the guy not to shoot him, he said, "I want to help your friend. Is he bleeding? Is he conscious?"

Darren licked his cracked lips. Despite himself, Rory recoiled from the spittle on the guy's mouth and a glimpse of his nicotine-stained teeth. Darren narrowed his eyes as he stared at Lise, ignoring Rory.

"Your gal pal can check on him, and then we're getting airborne." He shifted his weight from one foot to the other, his boots too big for him in the snow. "I'll take your gun, sweetie."

"Give him your gun," Rory whispered in her ear. "We've got our shotgun in the helicopter."

"Not a chance," she whispered back to him. "Are you crazy?"

A shotgun blast exploded to their right, snow and ice flying upwards and filling their vision.

"The next one goes in his stomach." Darren motioned toward Rory again with the end of the gun. "Hand over your weapon."

Lise removed her clip and handed him her gun. "Brilliant. All we need is more injured people." She walked right up to the convict as if daring him to shoot her, too.

"The ammo, too." Darren's bloody nose ran, and he swiped at it with his gloved hand.

"No." She handed him her gun, butt end first. "I'm going to check on your partner. If you shoot me in the back, or shoot him," she motioned towards Rory, "you'll have no one to fly this bird out of here. So, back up."

Rory's hands were still halfway in the air, the echo of the shotgun blast ringing in his ears. He didn't know where Lise's bravery was coming from, but he had to admit, it was more than a little attractive.

"Hey," he said to Darren, trying to catch his eye. "I'm getting that first aid kit now. We're going to see how bad Karl's hurt, okay?" He slowly backed up to the helicopter door.

Lise headed towards the plane crash, her boots crashing through the frozen layer of ice on top of the snow and forcing her to walk, tilting from side to side. They needed snowshoes, but none were on board.

He kept one eye on Darren, who kept swinging back and forth between the two of them, his shotgun wavering in circles. The first aid kit was strapped to the back wall behind the seats, and Rory struggled to get it down. He landed feet first, backwards out of the helicopter.

"Let's go see your friend," he said to Darren, who wiped his nose again and grunted.

"We're not friends."

"Okay," Rory edged up to him and stayed on the man's left side, away from the shotgun. He didn't trust the guy, and it would be suicide to try to disarm him in this deep snow. "You two escaped at the same time without a plan?"

"We had a plan." Darren's boots were collecting huge amounts of snow. They were obviously too big for him and belonged to someone else. "It was a brilliant plan. Until we wound up here. Stupid guy didn't calculate the fuel properly."

"That'll do it." Rory walked in front of the guy as they got near the crumpled front end of the small plane. The windshield and the pilot's door window were shattered. The left wing lay broken off about sixty feet away.

He could see Lise's flaming red hair inside the middle of the plane. Rory headed over towards her, even though Darren hadn't given him permission.

"Do you have a sling in that kit?" she called out through the broken window.

"I'm sure we do," he said, tromping through the ice crust, huffing as he got to the buckled metal door. "You guys were lucky. This could've been a lot worse."

The second convict threw him a hate-filled gaze. Lise was bent over at the waist and running her fingers along the other man's arm.

Lise motioned to Rory. "I need you to help me straighten out this fracture." She looked up into the convict's face. "This is gonna hurt."

"How do you know it's broken?" The man grimaced and pulled back his right arm. "You're no doctor."

"I can feel the two ends. They're side by side." She turned to Rory. "We can splint it, wrap it, and put him in a sling for now."

She'd removed the man's parka, and judging by his shivering, he was feeling the icy cold. Or going into shock. He wore a long-sleeved T-shirt she'd raised up over his elbow, and Rory could see the two lumps she was talking about... a nasty piece of business, but he could've broken his arm with much more damaging consequences. The guy was bleeding from a cut on his head, too.

Darren stood outside with the shotgun trained on all three of them. Rory stepped up into the small enclosure where the man was sitting against the wall of the crashed plane. He nodded at Lise.

"Alright, let's do this," he said. He put his hands under the man's forearm and elbow for support.

Lise gently put her thumb on the first bump under the skin and pushed backwards. Karl screamed. Rory hung on to his arm as the man bucked and banged his head against the metal wall in pain.

"Let me try to rotate it," she said, easing his forearm to the wrist. The bump was gone. Karl panted and screeched again.

"Nice work," said Rory.

"Grab what tensor bandages you have in that kit, and let's wrap it up." Lise leaned into Karl's face. "Immobilizing it will help with the pain. We'll give you whatever meds we have in the kit."

She eased his forearm up to ninety degrees from the elbow.

Rory passed her a tensor bandage and then held onto the man's fingertips. She began wrapping the bandage across Karl's palm and around his thumb, then around his wrist, and down around the forearm till she'd completely covered it. Then she tucked in the ends of the bandage at the top and bottom.

"Guess you do know what you're doing," Karl grunted.

"More'n anyone can say for you." Darren sniffed. He'd relaxed, the shotgun now pointed at the ground, his other hand on top of the doorway. "How stupid do you have to be to figure that fuel isn't measured in metric? It's gallons?"

Karl narrowed his eyes, and Rory jumped back despite himself. The escapee's sweat reeked of fear, anger, and the shock his body was dealing with. Rory watched the two men stare at each other, communicating without speaking, and wondered if there were any other guns deep in the plane's remains.

"Okay, let's go," said Darren, hefting the shotgun onto his hip. "Both of you can help him walk if he needs it. We're flying out before this storm gets here."

Rory stared past him at the snow beginning to fall sideways outside of the plane. He thought about the lack of response he'd gotten on the radio when he'd tried to call in the crash. These guys weren't the only ones stranded out here on the tundra.

Darren's hair stood up in frozen tufts, and he wiped his bleeding nose again. "I said, let's go."

"Help me stand. I can walk," said Karl.

"You need your jacket on. Neither of you are dressed for a blizzard," said Lise. "Or didn't you plan for the weather when you decided to do a jailbreak up north?"

"This idiot got us off course." Darren's face scrunched into a hateful mask. "Supposed to be a pilot. Couldn't even figure out that Yellowknife is west, not east."

Karl lunged to his feet. "Say that one more time, I dare

you!" He yelled again as his broken arm hit a piece of ragged metal. "If it weren't for me and my connections at the airport, you'd still be sitting in C block."

"Whoa, guys," said Rory. "We've got bigger things to worry about right now. There's a blizzard coming in. My helicopter radio may not be working." He realized he'd put his hands out in a supplicating gesture, while Lise stood by motionless. Watchful. "If we're all going to survive, we're going to have to work together," Rory said.

"Put this on," said Lise as she put Karl's jacket around his shoulders. He eased his good arm into it and then let her help him with the rest of it.

"See? That wasn't so hard," said Rory. "Darren, you're going to have to relax."

Darren worked up a gob of spit and hawked it onto the snow at his feet. The whirling flakes were coming down gently now, but that would soon change. Rory wanted to get back to some proper shelter. And the radio.

"Did you have any water or food in here?" asked Lise. She turned around in the small space. "Do you have flares or any survival equipment?"

Why hadn't he thought about that? He was the bloody pilot. All that was back in the helicopter were a couple more bottles of water and some granola bars. Maybe a flare, but this was the spare chopper, and he knew it hadn't been fully tricked out prior to their trip.

Well, that would teach him. There was never a *small* trip up north. He should've known better and been prepared. He swore under his breath.

"Flares, guys?" Lise demanded, her hands on her hips as the three men stared at her. "Blankets? Shovels?"

"Ask him," whined Darren. "He got us the plane from his *contact*. It was supposed to have everything we needed to fly to

Yellowknife. Instead, the idiot puts it on autopilot, going in the wrong direction, and we crash because they didn't put enough fuel on board!"

"Shut up!" roared Karl. "I swear I'll kill you if you open your mouth one more time." He turned back to Lise. "If there's anything like that, it'll be in the back of the plane. I didn't ask my buddy to load anything extra."

"Okay, let's check it out," said Lise, pushing past him. "We're going to need food and water, at least. And let's see if your radio's working before we leave this wreck."

Rory motioned to Karl to jump down ahead of him, and then he followed Karl. Lise sure knew how to take control of a situation. As the three men stood in the light snowfall, he wondered how she'd come up against a man she thought she couldn't marry.

Lise ducked her head to crawl inside what remained of the cockpit area. The plane was a four-seater, counting the two seats in the cockpit. Blood was splattered all over the instrument panel, likely from the two men falling forward in the crash and hitting it. Darren's bleeding from his nose and face was superficial, but Karl had a deep cut over his eye, although his major injury was his arm.

"I'm going to see if there's anything useful in here," she called out to Rory.

"Watch yourself. There's bound to be sharp pieces of metal sticking out, and we can't afford to have you injured," said Rory.

"I'm good," she yelled back.

She inched between the two mangled seats and poked around with her gloved hands to see if she could find any boxes or containers. Nothing. She reached forward, where the radio dangled from the right side of the instrument panel. The receiver box sat crushed underneath it.

"No radio here," she shouted over her shoulder. *Great. Here's hoping ours will work in this stupid storm.*

"Do you see a large, black switch marked ELT?" asked Rory. "It'll be on the dashboard somewhere."

She leaned over the front seat and spied a black lever to the left side. "There's some kind of lever-thingy that's in the OFF position," she said.

"Wow." Rory snorted. "Are there ARMED and ON markings there too?"

"Yes, do you want me to try and move it?"

"Push it to ON and see what happens," said Rory.

Lise had to shove it up with both hands because it had been smashed along with that section of the dashboard. Nothing happened.

"Did the light come on?" asked Rory.

"Nothing happened," she said. Tendrils of fear curled in the bottom of her stomach. Now, it definitely wasn't transmitting.

"It's okay," said Rory, "it might start transmitting eventually."

She slowly went back the way she'd come, watching not to snag herself on any of the projecting metal seat pieces. No radio, no extra supplies, and not even another first aid kit that she could see.

How am I going to get my gun back? She'd seen Darren put the gun in his left front pocket but doubted she could sneak it out without him feeling it. It was a miracle he hadn't followed through on his demand for the ammunition. She'd patted down Karl's jacket before helping him back into it, and at least he wasn't carrying a gun. Unless he had one in an ankle holster.

She turned around and took two seconds to search the rear of the plane. A pair of backpacks and a briefcase were all that was in the baggage area. She grabbed the backpacks and slung them over her shoulder and brought the briefcase out with her.

Lise jumped out of the side door and stood up in front of the three men, who looked like polar bears from the snow clinging to them. Darren grabbed the briefcase from her.

"I'll take that," he said, handing it back to Karl. "You can carry those..." He pointed to the black backpacks.

"What's in this stuff?" She tilted her head. "Anything we can use to survive out here?"

"None of your business," ground out Karl. "You ask too many questions."

She snorted and motioned towards the helicopter. The backpacks sagged like they weighed fifty pounds. She was dying to check what they were hiding.

"I'm no expert, but I don't think we're going to beat this storm," she said.

"Yes, we will," said Rory, his eyes on her, one eyebrow cocked. Was he trying to tell her something? "If we get moving right now, we can."

"Then get going!" Darren was getting on her last nerve. His whiney, nasal tone sounded like a cat in heat.

"After you, before we're completely covered in snow and ice," she said. She pointed at the helicopter. "You want to live? Let's go." As she passed the short man with the shotgun, she gave Rory a nod. If she got in first, maybe she'd get her hands on their shotgun stashed under the front seats. It only held cracker shells, but those would still scare the convicts.

She didn't wait for anyone to follow her but headed over to the helicopter. The wind whipped around her head, but if Rory thought he could fly in this, she had faith he could.

"Okay, okay, just let us in," said Karl. He held his right

forearm to his chest, and his face was scrunched up in pain. Lise could see he wasn't going to be any trouble. She reached her hand out to guide him forward and put her hands on his right shoulder.

"My partner is going to help me boost you up, okay? Put your foot up on the railing and get ready." She nodded to Rory, and then they both lifted Karl by the elbows. He held on to his broken arm and landed on his knees on the rear helicopter floor. He managed to edge forward and then used his left arm to haul himself into one of the seats.

She turned back to Darren, who still held the shotgun at the ready. He seemed uncertain about the climb up into the machine. Ice and snow covered his hair.

"You're going to freeze to death out here," she said. She waved him forward. "It doesn't matter to me if you die out here; it's totally up to you. This is your last chance to get inside."

Her little speech seemed to motivate Darren as he walked up to the open door and passed the shotgun through it to Karl.

"We're going to boost you up like we did your pal," said Lise. She put her hands out but didn't touch the short man, giving him some space.

Darren stared up at the doorway and gave them a nod. He wiped his nose and then reached for the sides of the opening. Rory and Lise put their hands under his elbows and heaved upward, using their shoulders to boost him into the small space. Once he was inside, Rory gave Lise a heave-ho, and she took the front left pilot seat.

Then, Rory pulled himself inside and hauled the door closed against the elements. It latched tightly, and now, they were inside a small tourist helicopter with two convicted murderers. The wind outside howled and buffeted the machine as the snow beat against it.

Lise turned in her seat and put her hand out to Karl. "I'm

going to need to put that shotgun up here for now," she said. "If we're all going to get out of this alive, you're going to have to trust us."

A look passed between Karl and Darren, a look she couldn't decipher but which didn't bode well. Anger flushed through her as she thought of her gun still inside Darren's jacket pocket. She wanted that shotgun, and she wanted it in her possession. The air seemed to vibrate with intense emotion between the two escaped convicts. Then Karl turned to her, holding the shotgun between his legs, and pointed up at the roof of the helicopter.

"I don't think it matters if it's up there or if it's back here," he said. His left hand tightened on the barrel. "Like you said, y'all are gonna fly us out of here. And then you're never going to see us again."

"Right," she said.

Lord, please let them realize at the airport that we're not back in time. Please keep us safe from these dangerous men, she prayed.

She huddled into her winter parka, crossing her arms and shoving her gloved hands into her sleeves. Rory reached over, his own furred mitt resting on her snow-panted leg. His touch reassured her, and his steady gaze helped to calm her heart rate.

Thank You, Lord, for this man. Thank You.

CHAPTER 7

The storm still blew a rush of wind sideways at them, but their breath, and the heat of their bodies, had formed a thick layer of condensation inside the helicopter windows. Rory swiped at the glass with his hands to peer outside.

"How about trying that radio again?" Karl pressed forward, his bad breath and body odour filling Rory's nose. The guy might be in pain, but his lack of hygiene was making Rory nauseous.

"If it didn't work a few minutes ago, it likely won't work now," said Rory, forcing a patience he didn't feel.

Oncoming storms sometimes affected the radio tower at the airport. He'd radioed several times when they'd first cozied up in here but received static for his efforts. That made Darren more anxious behind them.

"The airport knows we didn't get back in time," said Lise. "There'll be a rescue crew out looking for us soon."

No, no, no! Why are you saying that? Rory shot her a hard look with a quirked eyebrow, trying to convey a polite *shut-up* look.

"You need to get us out of here now!" Darren leaned forward and shoved Rory in the shoulder. "They train you guys to fly in all kinds of weather. Why else would you live up here in the back of nowhere?"

Karl pushed Darren out of the way and brought the shotgun into view between the two front seats. "We're not waiting around for any rescue crew. Get us airborne. Now."

The helicopter suddenly lurched to the right, shoving them up against each other. It creaked and groaned, plunging them together again. Lise grabbed Rory as she landed on top of him.

"What the heck?" yelled Darren as he hit the shotgun's barrel on his way to the floor.

"Bear," huffed Rory, as he grabbed for anything he could hold on to with his right hand while holding on to Lise with his left hand. "It's a polar bear. Stay still and don't move."

The bear's face appeared in the window of the side door. Lise twisted her head to the side and saw the massive bear's head taking up most of her vision. The beast stood against the helicopter and shoved it again with its front paws, making huffing sounds low in its throat.

"Do something! Get it off us!" screamed Darren.

"Shut up and lay still," Rory sputtered sotto voce. He sat against the right side of the helicopter.

The bear rocked back and forth on the machine, the crusted snow beneath them sickening in its creaking sound. When the bear put its nose to the door latch, Lise grabbed Rory's hand in a bone-crushing grip. The bear snuffled and bared its teeth at the latch, rumbling noises coming from its throat. Rory knew the bear saw them as tasty human treats inside a round toy and prayed under his breath that the wind would continue to gust hard against them.

Wait, he was praying now? Well, Lord, we haven't spoken in a while, but if You're around, now's the time for a miracle.

"Oh, dear Lord, dear Lord," Lise was praying out loud, still crushing his left hand with her own. She'd buried her head in his armpit. "Save us, save us, save us…"

The bear dropped to all fours. Rory forced himself to look up at the door window and saw the bear's shoulder roll away and out of his field of vision. More wind howled against the windows, the sound of its fury welcome in the absence of the bear's rumblings.

The four of them lay still for what seemed to Rory to be an eternity. The lilac smell of Lise's hair filled his nose, a welcome distraction from the body odour of the two convicts. Their hoarse breathing filled the helicopter, and Rory realized his own breathing was just as ragged.

Lise trembled against him. He pulled her tighter and let her bury her face against his neck. Sure, they barely knew each other, but given they'd been kidnapped at gunpoint and now nearly snacked on by a polar bear, he figured some comfort was in order.

"Is it gone?" Karl whispered. He was definitely the smarter one of the two.

"Let's hope so," said Rory, still making comforting circles with his hand on Lise's back.

"I need to get out of here," said Darren. He shoved himself back upright and reached for the "save me" bar on the left side of the helicopter. "I can't stay here anymore."

"No!" yelled Rory and Lise at the same time. She'd turned her head and then disentangled herself from their embrace. Rory struggled to regain his seat.

"No one's leaving. The only place you're safe right now is in here. That bear could be anywhere, but it's probably still nearby," said Rory.

"I'm claustrophobic," whined Darren. "I got the jitters. I'm going to lose it!"

"You're going to be fine, coz," said Karl.

This was the first time Rory'd heard either of them refer to the other with any kind of identification or endearment.

"You two are related?" Lise asked. Trust her not to miss a beat. Maybe now wasn't the time for an interrogation.

Darren clasped the "save me" bar with both hands, his eyes squeezed shut. "I ain't fine. I never should've listened to you." His whole body shook against the metal wall of the helicopter.

"Take some deep breaths," said Rory. "You're going to go into shock if you don't calm down."

"Yes, take some slow, deep breaths," echoed Lise. "Everything is going to be all right." She edged toward Darren. "I didn't know they put family together in prison. Did you guys ask to go to the same institution?" She reached up and put her fingers around his right wrist, which was closest to her. "I'm just going to take your pulse, okay?"

"We did a liquor store together." Karl grimaced as he held his broken arm. "Got twenty years, no parole, when the manager died."

Rory's stomach roiled as he caught another whiff of Karl's body odour. The man still clasped the shotgun in his weak hand, but Rory knew he had no chance of safely grabbing it in the tight space.

When the manager died... when you killed the manager more like...

"You're running fast," Lise said to Darren. "Take some more deep breaths. We don't want you getting shocky on us."

"We weren't together originally," Darren ground out. "I got transferred back from BC. Overcrowding from COVID." He blinked a few times, staring at Lise. "You ask a lot of questions."

"She's just making conversation," Rory interrupted. "We're all in this together."

"How about you try that radio again?" Karl's bald head

shone with sweat. "Don't say anything abnormal if you want your girlfriend here to keep enjoying living."

"Okay, okay," said Rory. "Stay calm." He picked up his radio mic again. "Churchill, JR one." More static. He keyed the mic again and repeated his call. Static filled the cockpit. "See? That storm's about to hit us, and it's interfering with my radio. We'd be idiots to fly with no radio."

Karl shoved the end of the shotgun behind Rory's ear. "Get us in the air before the storm hits, then. Do it. Now."

The cold circle of metal rested against Rory's skin. Funny how something ice cold could feel like a hot iron brand. His stomach dropped out, and he put his hands out slowly in front of him. "See? I'm not going to do anything stupid."

Lise sat stiff as a meerkat on a sand dune beside him.

"I'm going to flip the switches and get us in the air. Don't do anything rash." He prayed neither of them could see the minor tremor in his hands. He flipped the switches for the motor and the rotors and shot a glance over at Lise.

Her face as white as foolscap, she clenched and unclenched her fingers in her lap, staring forward out the window. No sign of what she was thinking.

"All right, here we go," he said, raising the collective lever to lift them up. The helicopter rose off the icy snow and swayed in the wind coming from the northwest. They'd be flying straight into it if they went to Churchill. He tried to think fast. What to do? Where to go that would be safe? Where could he get some help?

"We want to go to Iqaluit." Karl shoved the barrel of the shotgun against Rory's head again. "We can fly out of there, maybe to Europe. Take us there."

Europe? Was he crazy? Iqaluit was the capital city of Nunavut in the far arctic of Canada, on one of the arctic islands. The closest thing to Iqaluit was Greenland and then

Iceland before they'd ever be able to see Europe. These guys did not understand basic geography, and now he understood how Karl put the wrong airport code in his console for Yellowknife and flew the wrong way.

From here to Iqaluit was over fourteen hundred kilometres, and that was without a storm. His thoughts brought icy pellets of snow hurling against the helicopter. The visibility was poor, but he rose as high as he could to stay safe in the wind. He needed to avoid icing on the rotor blades, or they'd crash.

"Rory, this storm is going to get bad," Lise murmured under her breath, her mitten'd hand on his arm. He glanced over at her as he fought with the joystick to keep control of the aircraft. Her blue eyes had deepened to indigo—from the stress, he imagined.

"We need to head west. Goose Lake." She flicked her left thumb towards the left, out of sight of the convicts. "Cabins," she whispered.

Of course. The tourist campsite south of Churchill. They could break into one of the cabins and hide out for the duration of the storm. She was brilliant.

He nodded at her to show he understood and drifted the joystick in an arc to the left to change their course. Brilliant. What would happen when the two escapees realized they were still stuck in the wilderness? He had no idea, but for now, this was a genius plan. He flew straight west as the two men in the back argued between themselves.

They left the red and white plane behind them and flew on a diagonal into the oncoming storm.

Snow lashed at them as Rory fought to land the helicopter. The wind knocked them sideways, and Lise gripped the front edge of her seat with both hands. Adrenaline stormed through her veins as she prayed over and over in her mind. *God, don't let us crash. Don't let us crash. Please, please, please...*

They swirled to the right in a sickening half-circle and then landed with a bump. The wind heaved snow at them like a child in a snowball fight. Lise fell against Rory's shoulder and swayed sideways again. She was sure she'd left her stomach back up in the air. The blizzard roared and shoved the helicopter backwards, even though Rory had cut the engine.

They both unhooked their seat harnesses just as the left skid shifted and tilted sideways. The skid broke through the ice crust on top of the snow, falling a few inches into the drift.

Rory muttered a curse under his breath as Lise gasped. He tore off his headset. Lise lurched downwards against the glass door on the left side of the aircraft.

"I've got you," he said, as he finished undoing her harness and pulled her up towards himself.

"What happened?" She held onto the front of his parka as the helicopter shifted downwards again.

"There's more ice on top of this pack than I thought. The skids dipped into a drift that I couldn't see when I landed. Let's try to get out before anything else happens."

Lise put her hand around her eyes against her window and peered out. "I think we're on the ice of the lake, not the shore, don't you?"

"What ice?" barked Karl.

The helicopter shuddered and tipped on its side, the left-hand skid sinking even lower.

"Is that another bear outside?" screeched Darren.

"No bear; it's the storm. We've got to get into those cabins, or we'll freeze to death out here," said Rory.

Rory swung open his own door, which was tilted at an upward angle. He wiggled out and climbed down onto the skid, then jumped into the snow. Lise turned and came out backward into his arms.

"Whew! What now?" she said as she turned back to face him. Their breath mingled together in the frosty air, and snow swirled around their heads.

She could see vague outlines of wooden cabins through the blustery snow and ice. They'd made it to safety, but now they needed to get across to the buildings, break into one, and pray there were still some supplies from this year's campers.

"Thank goodness, we're back on solid ground." She blew out her breath. "And thank *you* for getting us here."

"Where is here?" Darren jumped down between her and Rory. "This don't look like no town. Where's the airport? We said we want to go to Iqaluit."

"There's no way we could fly that far in this storm." Rory reached up and ran his hand along the side of the half-sunk helicopter. "We'll be lucky to get this upright once the snow stops."

Karl poked the shotgun out the door and rested it on Rory's shoulder.

Lise turned before he could say anything. "Listen, you two. This blizzard is going to blanket us in deep snow for a couple of hours. Could even be a couple of days. We don't know." She tapped the end of the shotgun with her mittened fingers. "There's no point in trying to intimidate us because we know how to survive in this and you don't, so do what we ask, and we'll all get through this, okay?"

Karl grunted and pulled back the shotgun. Rory gave her an appreciative look, quirking his left eyebrow at her.

"Let's bring the food and water..." He motioned to the plastic grocery bag Karl held in his hand that held the water bottles and granola bars. "And you can carry your backpacks. Everyone put one hand on the shoulder of the person in front of you, and we'll head over to that cabin right there." He pointed to the nearest one.

Lise shivered, but not with the cold. They were only about thirteen kilometres south of Churchill, but no one knew where they were, and their helicopter was stuck. A tremendous blast of wind blew the three of them into each other just as Karl tried to jump down.

The helicopter's metal sides screeched as it gave way to the force of nature and landed fully on its side, the rotors touching the ice pack of the frozen lake.

"C'mon, we have to get to shelter." Rory's words were blown away, but she could read his lips.

She nodded her understanding as she grabbed the back of his parka and turned to Darren to motion to him to do the same to her. She leaned out and pantomimed to Karl to follow suit.

Heads down, the four of them put their bodies into the wind and pushed towards shore. Icy pellets pounded her face, stinging her skin like the giant black flies Churchill suffered from in July. Nature up here was always one extreme or the other.

Doggedly, she held on to her fist's worth of Rory's parka and followed his body into the maelstrom. The wind swept her breath away. Darren held her jacket in a tight grip, and she hoped Karl was managing with his one good hand. Rory stopped short, and she banged into his back, giving the bridge of her nose a whack. He reached back and grabbed her hand to steady her. He waved forward with his other hand, and she could pick out a wooden railing and steps partially obscured by snow.

As he went up the steps of the cabin porch, he stepped up and pulled her along. They all crowded together around the door, the wind howling like a Wendigo and swirling snow around them so hard she could barely make out the other two men. Rory fiddled with the doorknob, and it opened. Despair hit her. Did that mean there was nothing in it worth stealing? No supplies? No food left behind?

Rory yanked her into the cabin. Darren and Karl followed, and they stood shivering together. Rory thrust the door shut to keep out the snow. She was so cold. Bone deep cold. The cabin was pitch dark even though she knew it was still mid-afternoon. The sun wouldn't have set for at least another two hours except for the bitter storm outside.

"Where are we?" sniveled Darren.

"The bowels of hell," ground out Karl. He pitched forward into Lise's arms in a dead faint.

CHAPTER 8

The stench of Karl's body odour overpowered her as she lay pinned to the floor, his facial sweat tickling her nose and his heavy weight crushing her chest. She'd whacked the back of her head when they'd fallen together to the cabin floor, and sparkling stars wheeled across her eyes against the blackness of the overhead ceiling.

"Rory," she gasped.

The unconscious man must've weighed close to two hundred and fifty pounds. She heard Rory and Darren fighting in the darkness, grunts and shouted oaths going back and forth beside her. The two men crashed against furniture, and the sound of breaking pottery or glass echoed across the room.

"Argh!" roared Rory. He cursed again, yelling unintelligibly. "What did you do that for?"

She squirmed until she got her hands underneath Karl and pushed him twice until his comatose body rolled over enough so that she could wiggle out from under him. She could feel a goose egg forming on the back of her head. Rory was banging his boot against the floor and yelling.

Before she could go towards the sound of his voice, Darren grabbed the hood of her parka.

"Not a chance. You're going to help me find a light in this place." He hooked his forearm around the front of her neck and squeezed. "Do what you're told."

She felt the sharp edge of a blade against her throat. The nick in her skin began to bleed. Where was Rory? He sounded far away but was still moaning. Forcing herself to move with Darren, and keeping herself relaxed enough to be pliable, the two of them moved towards the left.

"Don't you want to check on Karl?" she asked.

"I don't care if he's dead. He's the whole reason we're in this mess." Darren tightened his grip on her neck. "Get over here. There must be cupboards somewhere."

"I think there's a window over there." She pointed with her right hand towards a lighter shadow. "Maybe we can see what the room looks like if we head over to it."

"Hmph," was all he said, but he pushed her forward into the lighter corner.

She was right. A frost-covered window hung over a kitchen sink. He shoved her up against the counter, knife still at her throat. For a second, his heavy breath in her ear and on the side of her neck felt like a dirty rag. His left hand came around the front of her parka, but which was still zipped shut.

She whispered thanks to God in her mind as his hand faltered and then dropped to her side again. She gripped the edge of the metal sink and wished she had a flashlight or anything she could turn into a weapon.

"Looks like that's a cupboard up there." He pointed to the left of the window. "Let's see what we can find. Move over here slowly, or you're going to get hurt like your hero boyfriend."

"Rory?" She was ashamed of her cracked voice the instant his name left her lips. "What did you do to him?" Anger swelled in her chest, even as the business end of the knife cut her skin. The thin line of blood trickled down her neck, but she didn't care. All she cared about was Rory and finding him in the dark.

"He's going to bleed out if we don't find some matches or a flashlight." Darren edged her along the counter. "Behave yourself, and maybe you'll have time to save him."

Lise put her hands outward on the counter, sweeping along it to feel for any objects. She hit round canisters. Reaching up, she hit pay dirt. Cupboards. With a small cry, she yanked open the first one with a handle and shoved her hands into the contents.

Coffee mugs clanked together. The sound of ceramics banging together set off heart palpitations. Why was it so dark? She gasped for air. The harsh wind swept around outside the cabin, throwing ice and snow at the window. If the drifts got deep enough, they could be buried alive.

"Noooo!" she shrieked along with the storm. Darren loosened his grip in surprise. She grabbed mugs and threw them to the floor. Running her hands inside the shelves, she reached up into the top of the cupboard. She hit a metal can, like a coffee can with a plastic lid. It flipped off easily, and her knees knocked together from relief when she felt the paper books of matches inside.

Squat candles sat beside the canister on the very top shelf. She pulled down every one she could reach and flicked several matches before she could light one properly. Her bare hands shook from nerves and the cold. When she'd lit five candles, the room flared into life with a warm glow.

Darren's knife hand dropped while she lit the candles. Karl had come to and lay on his back, staring at the ceiling and holding his broken arm. Rory sat against a fallen table, his left leg out to the side, pressing down hard on it.

"Oh my gosh, Rory! Are you okay?" She flew over to him, holding the candle high. "What did he do to you?"

"The stupid idiot knifed me in the thigh," Rory ground out. "I was trying to get the shotgun away from him."

"In the dark?" She knelt beside him.

"Not your brightest move," drawled Darren, standing in the middle of the room with said shotgun trained on them. "I believe we have a misunderstanding about how this is going to work."

"Yeah, how's that?" asked Rory as he grimaced in pain. Blood pooled under his thigh, soaking his jeans.

"Shut up, both of you! Let me think." Her heart pounded, roaring like a race car. Another injury, possibly a major one. She put the candle on the floor beside Rory and added pressure to the wound with her left hand.

"Look in the bathroom for something, anything, we can use to bandage him up," she ordered Darren.

Rory's face contorted in pain as he moved to lean against the couch, which had been shoved back in the altercation.

"Why me?" Darren's voice whined again.

"Because I'm holding back the blood pourin' out of him right now." She rounded on him, pushing down harder as she turned. Rory let out another gasp of pain. "Move it or shoot us right now. I don't care."

She vibrated authority. "Your buddy's half-passed out there, and now you've injured our only pilot. You. Are. An. Idiot." She spit out each word. "Find me something to bandage his leg with now."

With a shake of bravado, Darren swung the shotgun away from them and headed towards the bathroom. She could barely see beyond them. She'd been at these cabins last summer before she'd left for her supposed wedding and new life down south. They were only short-term rentals and hardly luxurious. A bedroom, bathroom, and main room, which included the kitchen essentials along the far wall.

Rory's breathing bothered her. Short, shallow breaths came from his mouth, and he kept pressing his lips together to hold in any exclamations or talk.

"Try to breathe normally," she said. "I need to look at how deep the cut is and where it is once that fool finds us something to bandage you up." She was crouched beside him and moved to a kneeling position. "What were you thinking?" she whispered in his ear, his hair tickling her nose.

"I saw an opportunity, and I took it." He took a shaky breath. "Should've figured he'd have a knife, the jerk."

"Did he stab you or slash you?" She kept her left hand pressed on his thigh and could tell the bleeding was stopping. Darren's crashing and banging around in the bathroom filled the small cabin.

"He slashed me twice," Rory said. "I didn't realize it at first until the last one. He really got me with that one."

"Hurry up," she yelled towards the bathroom.

Darren reappeared. "Or what? What you going to do, huh?"

He held the shotgun, pointing down to the floor by his right thigh. He also carried a couple of towels. She prayed they were clean and not rags he'd found.

"Why don't you check on Karl?" she said as she reached out to take the towels. "He's way too quiet over there. He probably has a concussion from smashing his head on the dashboard of the plane." She shook out a towel. In the semi-dark, she couldn't see what state it was in. "And why don't you try to find a light switch?" She knew she sounded exasperated but couldn't help herself. The guy was a donut short of a dozen.

"Because I'm guarding you two, so you don't come at us again." He sniffled, wiping his nose again.

She looked up and saw it was still bleeding. "Does he look like he's going to come at you? Find a light switch!" She leaned back on her heels. "These cabins all have electricity unless the storm's knocked it out. Man..." she said, as Darren moved toward the front door, "you sure have problems with authority."

"I have problems with women," he announced as he flicked the light switch, and the overhead light came on.

Lise sagged with relief. Now she could see Rory's pallor and the blood pooled over and under his jeans. Still, now she could get to work.

"Well, too bad. Check on Karl." She gingerly lifted her left hand from Rory's thigh wound. "Please," she said as Darren stood glowering at her, the shotgun now halfway from the floor to his waist. They stared at each other until Darren weakened and headed over to where Karl lay on the floor, still staring up at the ceiling.

"Check his pupils and see if you can get him talking," she ordered. Then she leaned into Rory and said, "It's going to hurt, but I've got to lift the material to see what the wound looks like... I wish I had small scissors or a first aid kit, but I don't..."

Rory cracked her a half-smile, half-grimace. "I'm going to be fine. I've got a jackknife in my right front pocket. Use that to cut my jeans."

"You're sure?"

He nodded and then leaned his head back against the couch again. She cast a glance over at Darren and then surreptitiously reached into Rory's front parka pocket and felt around for the jackknife.

It was a beauty. Carved bone handle with two blades. She held it in awe. Then she flicked open the bigger of the two blades, trying to keep it out of Darren's field of vision.

"It's exquisite, for a knife," she whispered in his ear. "Where did you get such a unique one? Is that a polar bear carved into the side of the handle?"

"What are you two whispering about over now?" demanded Darren.

She palmed the knife. "Nothing. I'm trying to get him to breathe easier. How's Karl?"

"How should I know? I'm no doctor, and neither are you," he sniveled.

"No, but my first aid training is all we've got," she said. "How are his pupils?"

"They look normal to me," the redneck convict said.

"Okay, let me finish with Rory, and I'll come over and see him. Why don't you check the cupboards for any food the renters might've left behind?"

She might as well be dealing with a five-year-old. She flicked open the knife again and carefully started cutting Rory's jeans upward from the biggest rip from Darren's knife. It sliced through the material so fast she almost nicked herself. Darren wandered over to the long countertop that held the kitchen stove and bar fridge and began banging the cupboard doors.

"This is a dangerous knife!" She cut the side of her opposite index finger and sucked on it in pain. She rolled her eyes at Rory, trying to make him laugh, but got nowhere.

"Dad gave it to me when I was thirteen." He blew out his breath. "Said I was a man now and cut me across my palm with it to show me how sharp it was... is." His fingers enclosed the wrist of her sore hand. "Sorry, I should've warned you." His touch warmed her all the way to her shoulder.

"No worries." She leaned forward and pulled the material apart to better see the wound. A large, ragged gash that looked to be about five inches long and was still seeping blood. She gently pressed down on one side to see how deep it was, making Rory exhale loudly.

"You're going to think I'm some kind of weakling for sure." He grunted. "I'm sure once the bleeding stops, I'll be okay."

She snorted. "Aidan would've been incapacitated by a paper cut. I would've paid to see him try to tackle some guy with a shotgun." Rory's amber eyes were staring at her, and she blushed. The embarrassing warm flush swept from her neck upward over her cheeks and freckles. Mortified, she reached for the towels.

"Those smaller cuts need butterfly bandages. I need a first aid kit or super glue or something..." She shoved her hair back over her forehead.

"Our first aid kit is somewhere in the helicopter out on that pond," he whispered. "Tie a towel around the worst of it, and I'll try not to move too much for now."

She made quick work of the make-shift bandage, tying it with the knot over the open wound. Helpless, that's how she felt, and it made her angry. Angry at these two losers who'd kidnapped them and angry at their situation. Being thirteen kilometres away from town without a radio or working phone might as well be a hundred kilometres.

The storm still raged outside, the wind battering at the few windows. She muttered a prayer of thanks under her breath for the electricity.

"You still believe in God after everything you've been through?" Rory's clear amber eyes, laced with red lashes, took stock of her still-flushed face. "D'you really think He had anything to do with the power being on?"

"We're having theological discussions now, are we?" She tried to sound light, even though anger clogged her throat. "You know what they say, there're no atheists in foxholes. And," she continued, as she settled down beside him, "this is certainly a foxhole."

"Enough!" roared Darren. He shoved her shoulder with the front end of the shotgun. "I don't know what you two are babbling about, but how about you fix us something to eat?"

"Watch it." Her heart thrummed as she looked sideways at the shotgun. "If you take me out with that thing, you'll definitely be on your own here."

"I'm hungry. Karl's awake." Darren wiped his nose with the back of his hand, then motioned toward the cupboards he'd opened. "There's some canned tuna and macaroni kits over on the counter. Get something going so we can eat."

"As soon as I check on Karl," she said, slowly standing up with her hands out in front of her. Not quite in supplication, but not backing down, either. "I'll fix us something hot if the stove works. Meantime, can you see if there's any extra blankets?"

"What for?" Darren was already heading for the countertop, hitching up his pants as he walked.

"In case the power goes out with the blizzard, we should have blankets handy to keep us warm. There're no fireplaces in these cabins because the firepits are outside."

Karl moaned from the floor and tried to turn onto his side. She went over to him and crouched down low again, feeling his forehead with her right hand.

"Just checking you for fever," she said. "How's your head? Any headache? Nausea?"

"Hurts some," he croaked out. "Fell asleep there. My arm and shoulder are killing me. Where's the pain pills?" He sat up with the help of his good arm.

"We brilliantly left the first aid kit out in the helicopter," she said. "You'll have to make do."

He swore loudly and with imagination.

"I'm worried you've got a concussion or worse," she said. "Let me know if your head hurts more or you feel faint again." She held his eyelids open on both eyes and checked his pupils for herself. They seemed a bit dilated. "I've got two of you in pain, thanks to your magnificent cousin over there." She pointed toward Darren. "Swear at him, not me. I'm going to try to fix us some kind of meal."

She picked up the grocery bag of water bottles and granola bars and ignored Darren and his shotgun as she headed to the countertop. He'd clumped cans of tuna and two boxes of macaroni together. Lise picked up the cans and checked the expiry dates on them. They were good.

She flung open the other two cupboard doors to check for any pots to boil water. This was a bare bones rental. People were told to bring their own supplies, which was why the cabins were so cheap. Granola bars and tuna. *Well,* she thought to herself, *at least it's not cold, canned beans.*

The last cupboard held one banged-up pot with a loose handle. She brought it down and ran the tap over the sink. The pipes rattled, but nothing came out. Tears pricked her eyes in frustration. The pipes chugged and gurgled, and finally, a trickle of water came out. She held the pot under the tap, hoping to get enough to boil up some macaroni for a hot meal.

The wind still howled outside. The log walls weren't insulated, and she knew they were risking hypothermia. Water gushed forth after the pipes gave one last burble. She filled the pot, thankful for the precious water, and headed over to the stovetop.

Please keep the electricity going, she prayed under her breath. *Please let them know back home that we're still out here.*

CHAPTER 9

Rory's right leg throbbed with pain. His left shoulder wasn't much better. He could tell his shoulder was half out of its socket. Excruciating pain flared down his arm, and he bit his lip again to prevent making a sound. He'd watched Lise boil water and macaroni noodles and monitored the two convicts from his spot on the floor.

When she gave them each a bowl of tuna and noodles, he shifted so he could keep Darren in sight. Her breath plumed in the freezing air as she whispered to the two escapees. He was nauseous from the pain and adrenaline knifing through his body.

Lise took two small bowls from the counter and sidestepped over the other two men. She sat down beside him on his good side, away from his injured leg, and offered him the bowl of food with a spoon.

"I need you to help." He turned his face away from the others. "Can you pop my shoulder back in?"

"Your shoulder? Why didn't you say something?" Her eyes widened. "Which one?"

He briefly shut his eyes. *God, will this nightmare never end? Can something please go right for us?*

"Shhh... it's my left one," he whispered. "Do you know how to do it?"

"Yes, of course." She cast a glance at the convicts, who were noisily slurping down their macaroni and tuna. "Can you lie down? Or do you want to try it sitting up?"

"I'll sit, thanks. I don't want to telegraph to them I'm more injured than they already think."

Lise nodded and then reached for his waist. "Don't worry, I'm going to undo your belt and slide it off so I can use it for a sling." She smiled at him, her face so close he could've leaned forward a couple of inches and planted a kiss on her cheek. Her hand flipped open the leather tongue in his belt buckle, and even in his pain, he wanted to laugh at their predicament.

They'd gone way beyond the parameters of a first or even second date. After this experience, would she even want to go out with him if he asked her to?

She gently pulled on the belt, and he tried to shift his weight from side to side to allow it to release from his belt loops. Her other hand went behind his waist, and her fingers wrestled with a bit that didn't want to come loose.

He snorted a laugh despite himself.

"You think this is funny?" Her hair was in his nose, and even now, her curls smelled of fresh snow, flowers, and her... he must be getting delirious. "Shh..." she whispered.

The belt was free, and she drew it into loops in one hand. "Okay, try and sit up as straight as you can. I'm going to hold your arm out straight in front of you." She put the belt on her lap and held his wrist in both hands. "I'm going to pull forward and try to straighten your arm. If this doesn't work, you're going to have to lie down for me."

He had no arm; it was pure throbbing agony she was holding. He bit his lip and tasted blood on his tongue. Nodding, he screwed his eyes up tight.

Rory's upper body followed his arm forward, and the ball of his shoulder popped and then fell back in. Her relocation of the joint was over in seconds, and the pulsating up-and-down pain subsided to a centralized pain. He flopped back against the upturned couch with a groan.

Lise slid the belt around the back of his neck and eased him towards her. She positioned it across his shoulder blades and put his arm across his chest at the same time. Then she did up the belt, tightening it enough to support the arm in place. She sat back on her feet to admire her handiwork.

"If you ever decide you don't want to deal with wild animals anymore, I'm sure you could get a job at the Health Centre as a nurse," Rory moaned. "Thank you. That's better." He sagged against her, and his heart pounded against her hand.

"I want to check your leg wound again, see if it's bleeding," she said.

Her body heat was enticing. She'd loosened her parka earlier, and her flannel shirt and turtleneck smelled like fresh linen and lilacs. He was tempted to stay pressed together for warmth, but she moved to his other side and checked the bandage for seepage.

"I don't feel any fresh blood. It seems dry. That's good."

"Good. D'you still have my knife?"

"Yes," she said, reaching for her front pocket," d'you want it?"

He put his hand over hers and held it, holding it away from her parka, and gripping it tightly. "No, keep it in case you need it."

"Need it?" She barely breathed the words. "I'm not going to use it on one of them." She tossed a quick glance over at Karl and Darren, sitting in two over-stuffed chairs, eating their makeshift supper. "I can't just stab someone. Shooting a person is one thing. Stabbing them is quite another."

"Yeah, you might feel differently depending on the situation," Rory said. "Keep it hidden. Just in case."

He kept his hand over hers and drew her down close beside him. "I hate to be a bother, but can you help me eat that?" He jerked his chin towards the bowl on the floor beside them. Her hand was hot and strong in his own. Her body heat flared like a furnace, and all he wanted was to lie down beside her and fall asleep. That showed how dangerous his body condition was, and he knew better. He needed to eat and drink and get warmer.

"Of course. I'm sorry!" She shifted forward, but he kept her hand, forcing her to look back at him. Her blue eyes, with those indigo rings around the irises, shone in the overhead's glare light bulb. Intelligence, empathy, confidence; she poured everything into that glance. His stomach bottomed out in a good way.

"Shh," he whispered as he pulled her back to him. She folded into him like a glove, their foreheads touching. The tip of her nose grazed his, its freezing tip echoing the shivers in his own body. Their breath fanned together. Her lips grazed his, and then she moved infinitesimally to reach them full-on. Her kiss was like life stirring his blood, and he kept hold of her hand as if he could keep her there forever.

She made a tiny sound in the back of her throat and rested her forehead on his again. They breathed each other's air for a few seconds. The pain in his leg and shoulder didn't matter. Nothing mattered but her and keeping her safe.

"Lise," he said.

"Hey! I told you two to cut it out." Darren jumped to his feet and leveled the shotgun at them. "I'll tie you both up. Get back." He kicked Lise's feet.

"Whoa." She sprang to stand. "Touch me again, and you're going to need more than that shotgun." Her hands were out at her waist, but Rory could see she was balanced on the balls of her feet. "You hear that wind howling outside? This blizzard isn't going anywhere. We're all stuck with each other."

"Sit down, Darren," said Karl. "She's right. You ate, didn't you?"

"You shut up," Darren yelled at Karl. "It's your fault we're in this godforsaken place. You put the wrong airport code into the autopilot. Your so-called friend didn't load enough fuel on board." He hitched the shotgun to his shoulder and pointed it at Karl, who still sat in the ancient brown chair. "I should kill you right now."

Karl's eyes glittered in the LED overhead light bulb of the cabin. "That's your solution to everything—shoot anything that moves. I can't believe Ma bailed you out so many times over the years."

Rory's stomach roiled. Lise put her hands on her hips.

"That's right. You two are cousins, right?" She shifted her stance, and Rory could see she was in Darren's line of peripheral vision.

Please God, don't let him shoot, prayed Rory.

"Family comes first," she said as she edged inch by inch to the right. "Karl, your mom must've believed in Darren if she bailed him out of trouble."

Rory could see the sweat beaded on Karl's bald head. Karl sounded brave, but he obviously knew his cousin's propensity for violence as he sat like a statue.

"We took him in when he was four years old. Our mothers were sisters," said Karl through clenched teeth. "His mom died..."

"Don't you talk about my mother," screamed Darren.

"Okay, okay, let's all take a breath here," said Lise. Her hands were out in an entreating gesture. "We've had a hot meal, and we have a roof over our heads. I say we find any blankets or other stuff we can use to stay warm and call it a night."

The change in tone and words diverted Darren enough to set his hands trembling on the shotgun. His face contorted until Rory realized he was crying. Karl still sat with his hands up in a surrendering position.

"Darren, let's check the other room for blankets, or even sheets," Lise said soothingly. "It's all right. It's going to be all right."

Darren lowered the shotgun and wiped his nose. "I don't need your help. I'll find them myself." He swung around and marched towards the bathroom and single bedroom.

Rory let out his pent-up breath. A bum leg and shoulder. He tamped down the anger at the whole situation. How was he supposed to help Lise in this condition?

Karl slumped forward in his chair, holding his bandaged arm with his other hand. "Thank you," he said to Lise. "He's always been a freak. His mom was beaten to death in their apartment, and no one found them for almost a week." He paused, looking toward the bedroom. "Firefighters were called because Darren tried to make spaghetti and boiled the pot dry, so it set off the fire alarm."

"And he was only four years old?" Rory exclaimed.

"Yeah, he thought his mom was sleeping, so he wanted to wake her up and make her dinner." Karl blew out another breath.

"Did they ever find her killer?" Lise whispered.

"No, it was probably one of her drug buddies." Karl's hands shook.

"You really thought he was going to shoot you," said Rory.

"He shot the liquor store manager," said Karl. "He didn't have to; we could've gotten away. He just did it. Said he felt like it, so he did it." Karl wiped the sweat from his face with his one good hand. "I thought I was a goner, so thank you."

Rory didn't miss the pallor of Karl's face. Lise could be

right. He probably did have a head injury. They were both nearly out of commission, leaving Lise to hold back Darren's hair-trigger temper. And just because Karl shared family history with Darren, didn't mean he was trustworthy, either.

Darren appeared with an armful of bedding. He dropped it in the middle of the floor, still babying the shotgun with his strong arm. "This is it from the bedroom. There's nothing else in the closet." He glared at Lise. "How do you figure these sheets are going to do anything?"

"They're an extra layer of warmth," she said. "Give one to Karl and use one for yourself."

"Why? You want to make sure we survive so you can turn us over to the cops?"

"I want to make sure you survive so your death isn't on my conscience," she said, pulling a ratty-looking blanket towards herself. "We'll use this one."

She scootched backwards towards Rory with the blanket, never taking her eyes off Darren. She handed one end to him and began spreading it over their legs.

"Aw, like you care." Darren snorted. He rolled his eyes as he leveled the shotgun at the two of them sitting up against the couch. "I'm so touched. Ain't you the biggest liar on planet earth."

"Seriously, dude," said Rory. "Can you put the shotgun down? No one's going anywhere."

Darren snapped the shotgun's front end up vertically. "You got that right. Get some sleep. Then we'll see who really knows how to survive in this godforsaken place."

Rory's leg was on fire, but his arm was down to a dull throb. He reached behind Lise with his good arm and pulled her closer to him for body warmth. To his relief, she sank against him and brought the lightweight blanket up over his chest.

She brought her lips close to his right ear. "Stay warm. If he falls asleep, I'm going for that shotgun."

CHAPTER 10

"You two want to talk all night, you can do it in there." Darren gestured with the shotgun toward the one bedroom. "I want to sleep."

Lise stared up at him and calculated how fast she'd have to move to grab the gun and overpower him. Now that her bottom was flat on the floor, she'd limited herself. Rage poured adrenaline through her veins. It was a welcome relief from the frozen temperature in the cabin.

"Get up." He kicked her boots. "Y'all can get moving. Now."

"I told you not to do that," she spat out.

"Lise," Rory whispered, "let's do what he says."

"No." She didn't want to be cut off from the food and water supply. Surely, Rory could see that? "We're fine where we are."

"Get up," Darren repeated, "or I'll take out his other shoulder."

"Okay, okay." She thrust her hands forward in submission. "We're going. Let me help him up." She gathered the blanket and rolled onto her feet. Without taking her eyes off Darren or the shotgun, she gave Rory her strong hand.

Rory cursed under his breath. He rolled onto his good hip

and got that leg under him. He let Lise steady him with her right hand and pull him upward. His belt held his left arm and shoulder in place.

"Move it," said Darren.

Lise peeked over at Karl, who'd wrapped himself up in a sheet and covered his head with it. He looked like an oversized silkworm sitting in the chair. She could see him shivering. She took Rory's arm with her one hand and hiked up their blanket with the other one.

Furious, she could feel the hot rush of anger flushing her face as they stepped into the small bedroom opposite the one washroom. It held a double-sized bed, a dresser with three drawers, and one night table with a lamp. A single window with blue cotton curtains was covered in frost. Not exactly the lap of luxury, but these cabins were for summer tourists who wanted to explore the native tundra and see the wolves and polar bears inland.

Darren grinned at them with his crooked teeth and slammed the door in their faces. She leapt forward to open it, but he held on to the doorknob from the other side. He cackled as she desperately tried to turn it.

"Get some sleep, princess." He laughed.

She tried again to turn the door handle. "Has he taken the knob off?" She yanked backwards on the knob. Hot tears came then, coursing down her face and blurring her vision. The room had no lights. Pitch dark and all she could hear was Darren's hooting laughter in the other room, along with the whistling of the blizzard around their windowpane.

"Lise, come here," said Rory. "You're going to break it."

His voice sounded powerful coming out of the darkness. He sounded... fierce. Was this the guy she'd just helped limp in here? Maybe she was delirious. Maybe this had all been a nightmare, and she'd wake up in her tiny, two-room apartment on Kelsey Boulevard. She'd laugh about the bad dream with Braden over their morning coffee before work.

"Lise, come here," said Rory. He was sitting on the bed. She could sense his presence in the dark. "We need to stay warm. We're going to be fine."

We're going to be fine... since when? No one knows where we are...

The doorknob jumped beneath her hand. "There, now you won't bother us with your yakking." Darren moved away from the door as she pounded on it. He'd jammed a chair or something under the doorknob.

She screamed and hammered on the door with both hands, every piece of her frustration slamming into the wood.

Rory's body warmth enveloped her from behind as he grabbed one of her hands and held it still above her head.

"Shhh..." He breathed against her ear. "Shhh..."

She trembled like a newborn foal, tears flowing, stomach clenching, her head screaming.

He brought her hand down and turned her body around, leaning her gently against the door. His thumb and forefinger found her hot tears and wiped them away. Her eyes swam with salty tears. She couldn't stop.

"Don't give him the satisfaction," he whispered. His lips pressed a slow, gentle kiss to her forehead. Her heart still thrummed against her ribs, but her breathing slowed as he put his forehead on hers.

Those tears fell again, and she couldn't stop them. His lips whisked them from her cheeks. His breath warmed her body down to her toes. She didn't dare move in case she missed a sensation.

"You've been so brave. You can take a break," he said. His beard scruff wiped away the last of her tears. She wanted him to kiss her properly, but he seemed to hold back. Acting like a gentleman even in their life-and-death situation.

"I don't feel brave," she said as he peeled her from the door and moved her toward the bed. Her eyes adjusted to the darkness, and she could see the shapes of the furniture even though the door was shut.

"You're the bravest person I've ever seen." He sat her down and wrapped the thin blanket around her. "I can't believe how you've stood up to Darren."

She shivered, but not from the cold. She felt, rather than saw, her breath plume in the air of the small bedroom. "Fat lot of good it's done us. I didn't get my gun back. We're locked in here." She leaned against him, her head on his good shoulder. "What if they leave us here? We'll freeze to death, and they won't find us till next July when they open the camp."

"They won't leave us here," he said. His voice rolled over her like hot toffee. "They need us to figure out which way to go when the storm blows out."

"D'you think so?"

"I know so," he said, wrapping his good arm around her. "These guys have zero geography smarts. They think they can get on a boat and sail to Europe through Hudson Bay."

"What?" She couldn't keep the shock out of her voice. "And what boat do they think they're going to get in Churchill to cross the ocean, even if that were possible?"

"That's what I mean. They have no idea what they're doing. All we have to do is play along with their stupid idea and get ourselves back to town." He kissed the top of her head. "Let's get this blanket around you, and we'll try to get some sleep."

"You need to stay warm, too. You're the injured one," she said.

"I'll be plenty warm up against you."

She could hear the smile in his voice, even in the dark. "And I promise to be the perfect gentleman."

Lise felt him moving over on the mattress and then tugging on her blanket.

"How's your shoulder?" she asked as she scooted over to lie beside him, the blanket enveloped around her.

"It's fine. I can manage the pain," he said. "I took off the belt sling so I can use my arm if I have to." He pushed the one pillow under her head. "Get comfy."

"It's good if you can still feel some pain," she said as she nestled in beside him. "That means you're not getting hypothermic. That's the last thing we want." She caught a faint whiff of his sandalwood beard oil. "I still think you should have some of this blanket, too."

"I'm good," he said. "I've got extra layers on, and we're pressed up together."

His body heat was warming her up. She snuggled in closer and put her arm across his chest. "You asked me if I still believe in God after everything that's happened," she said.

"You still believe in God now, when we're being held hostage?" he asked.

"Of course." She tucked her gloved hand into the blanket. "Losing my temper doesn't mean I don't believe God is here with us."

"Hmph..." Rory made a noise above her head, where he was resting his chin.

"You don't believe He knows what's happening to us?" she pressed.

"I think that's kind of a Sunday School way of looking at it," he said slowly. "I'm not sure God is omnipresent in people's lives like some people think."

"What do you mean?"

He pulled her closer to him, and she tucked her face in against his shoulder.

"I guess I never got a straight answer to why God lets bad things happen to good people." He snorted. "Take us, right now. Why did God let this happen to us? And why did God let my father drown all those years ago?"

"Maybe God let this happen to us because we're the right people to deal with it," she whispered.

"The right people?"

"Yes, we have the skills and survival knowledge," she said.

"We have a crashed helicopter and some canned tuna in an unheated cabin in a blizzard."

"We have the smarts to deal with these guys," she tried again. "What if they'd taken tourists hostage and shot Lukas Tanner from Guiding Star? Tourists would've likely perished already."

"You might have something there," he said. "Lukas got shot a couple of years ago, though. He's pretty hardy stock."

"I'm sorry about your dad," she said. She heard his heart beating underneath her cheek. She'd slowly inched over onto his chest and took comfort in the warm flannel of his shirt. "But we don't know why God lets bad things happen to us. Just that He's always with us and will get us through them."

His body stiffened.

I'm such an idiot, she thought. She raised her head in the dark, even though she couldn't see his face clearly.

"Sorry, *that* sounded like a Sunday School answer. I've never lost someone I love to death. Yet."

Rory lay staring up at the ceiling. His muscles were rigid, but he kept his good arm around her. "My dad drowned in an accident on a bright, perfect July day. A couple of tourists panicked in their kayaks when some beluga whales got too close to them. He tried to help, but they capsized his, too, and he couldn't get upright again." His heart beat a tattoo under her palm on his chest. "He drowned underneath their paddles and kayaks. I couldn't reach him in time."

Words choked in her throat. Nothing seemed adequate to rise to the picture she saw in her mind of the Churchill River with thrashing, panicking tourists in kayaks. How many times had she been on the river herself, enjoying the company of the belugas? It was one of summer's greatest pleasures up north.

"I'm so sorry, Rory," was all she could say. She hugged him closer.

"Where was God then?" he whispered in the dark.

"I don't know," she said.

He was right. Where was God? Why did a good man die for nothing? She'd never once considered such a question.

"I haven't been out on the river in seven years," he said. "I can't face it. My mom says I have to, but I can't do it." He squeezed her with both arms. "I can't breathe if I stand on the docks."

"Like you're having a panic attack," she said, not caring that he was cutting off her breath with his embrace. Somehow, she knew he'd never spoken of this to anyone before.

"Yeah, maybe," he ground out. "All I see in my mind is my dad's head disappearing under the waves and not coming up again."

"Did you ever...?" She stopped herself. How rude to ask such a question.

"Recover his body? Yeah, a few days later, the RCMP found him with some luck. The tide brought him in." He stopped talking for so long that she was afraid to say anything else. "The whole town came out for his funeral. It was good for Mom; she needed the support."

All she could do was hug him back. Where were her pat

answers about God in the face of such raw grief? Seven years later, and he sounded as if his dad had died a few days ago.

"I'm afraid to go to sleep," she finally said. "I don't want to freeze to death."

"We're going to be warm enough," he said. "And we can break that window come morning if those two losers don't let us out of here."

"If you're sure," she said. She was afraid of the lethargy crawling over her arms and legs. It would be so easy to fall asleep and never wake up. Her body was relaxing, and that might be dangerous.

He kissed the top of her head again.

I wish he'd kiss me properly, was her last thought as sleep claimed her.

Rory's leg and shoulder pain kept him awake, and that was fine by him. He wanted Lise sharp for their next session with their captors, and she needed the sleep. As long as she was breathing evenly in his arms, he knew she was all right.

His eyes adjusted to the darkness in the room. He'd spent some summers as a kid down at this camp and knew his way around the cabins. If the blizzard blew itself out by daylight, their biggest problem would be getting back to the helicopter and seeing if they could turn over the engine to raise the radio. If not, they'd have a long walk north, back towards Churchill in the snow.

He strained to hear anything on the other side of the thin wall from the other two men. If they froze to death, that would solve half of their problem, but he wasn't wishing death on them. Not even on Darren. The two men deserved to go back to prison for their crimes, which now included jailbreak and their kidnapping. That he was looking forward to—turning them over to his brother-in-law, Constable Ben Koper.

Seven years had passed since he'd been in a life-and-death situation on the river with his dad. Now, he was in another one, but this time, he had the resources to make a difference. Not the physicality—Lise was the only one not injured—but he knew they made a good team. They were better together.

That thought stopped him cold. He'd been a lone wolf, as Adam called him, for all his life. The responsible older brother who kept his mother's Café running when his dad died. The older brother who gave up on his own dreams of moving south to let his little sister go off to Winnipeg on a lark. He'd stayed behind and slung eggs and hash for his mother, kept the books, and kept her fed when she would've descended into grief so deep, he feared she needed to be hospitalized.

Lise's even breathing warmed his neck as he held her close in the dark. He'd told no one how his father really died. A bigger boat had rescued the tourists involved. They'd absolved themselves of responsibility, loudly threatening to sue the tour guide company for their distress and terror.

He'd been left on the river in his own kayak, paddling back and forth, desperately trying to show the RCMP officers in their boat where his dad had gone down. His father's kayak bobbed at the surface, a vivid green conveyance that mocked his attempts at diving several times beneath the waves.

The RCMP Corporal had grabbed his T-shirt when he came up for air and insisted he get back into his kayak, which they had tied to their bow. The freezing air around him now felt the same as the freezing water he'd endured trying to find his father beneath the rolling whitecaps on the river.

He let the memories wash over him. He'd kept his mother mercifully ignorant of the involvement of the other people in her husband's death. A heart attack was the story he came up with so that she could have some comfort. But whether his dad died from human error or a medical emergency, he still didn't see God's presence in that day.

His chest muscles had relaxed, he realized with a start. His breathing was normal, and yet his memories of that horror had overcome him completely. Lise's arm lay over his chest, her head resting on his good shoulder. She fit beside him like they were made for each other.

Well, God, he thought, *if you're really here, I'm glad she's with me. Glad she wasn't flying with John McIsaac.*

He chuckled to himself. John wouldn't have tried to tackle Darren and wouldn't have gotten himself knifed. John would've had the good sense to keep his hands in the air and do whatever he was told to do. He was a great bush pilot but not known for his bar fighting abilities. Rory, on the other hand, had definitely been in a few fights in his youth.

Lise hadn't mentioned the flowers. She wasn't like any other woman he'd dated in his teens or before his dad died. That was his life—a before and after—cut in two by his father's death. He was one way beforehand, carefree, and not even looking to stay in the northland. And then he'd been thrust into the role of an adult, taking care of everything his dad did for the family.

In the dark, he promised himself he would get her back to Churchill in one piece. Even if they had to ditch their unwanted sidekicks in the wilderness. He snorted. Not very Christian of him, and his mom wouldn't like that thought, which was why he kept that dark part of himself locked away. Most people didn't deserve second chances, especially when they'd proven what they were made of in the first place.

Lise muttered something in her sleep and shifted her head. She was all that mattered to him. He might've failed his father, but he wasn't going to fail her.

CHAPTER 11

Lise woke up before Rory and grimaced at her aching left shoulder and arm from lying in one position all night. She inhaled their combined body heat and gently rested her open palm on his chest to feel his heartbeat again. Its regular tempo reassured her.

Utter silence bore down on the cabin. No more rushing wind outside, no more ice pellets against the windowpane. She strained to hear any sound from the next room, but there was nothing. No sign the two convicts were still present.

She didn't want to wake Rory, but she needed to use the facilities and wanted to scope out where Darren and Karl had gotten to. His good arm made it awkward to untangle herself from his embrace in the dim morning light. She edged backwards slowly and hauled her blanket up and over his sleeping form on the bed.

The window was frozen shut. Deep frost filled the glass pane, and the inside sliding panel was definitely not going to move. She took out his bone-handled knife and tried to dig at the inches-thick ice but realized it would take forever to free up the whole window. She had no exit that way.

She hit a couple of creaks on the wooden floor but reached

the bedroom door. The handle turned without a problem, no longer jammed from outside. Had the two convicts had a change of heart and left them behind but given them an escape route? She leaned against the door, straining to hear anything on the other side.

Rory's soft breathing filled the room. She took a chance and turned the knob. The bathroom across the hall was empty. She stepped into the short hallway and looked to her right, towards the main room. Nothing. Not a sign of the other two men.

Her pressing need for the bathroom won out. She finished up and washed her hands, determined to get outside and over to the helicopter to see if her portable radio still worked. Once she eased her way into the living room, she saw that the two escapees had left their blankets on the chairs but were nowhere in sight.

No one had made any attempt to make breakfast. The men were gone. Had they gone for the disabled helicopter as well? She zipped up her parka and donned her fur hat and gloves. Rory still slept, but she would be quick.

The sun on the snow blinded her when she opened the cabin door. Her sunglasses were in the downed helicopter as well. She searched in her front pocket for Rory's knife, her only weapon. She'd feel a lot better if she had her gun back in its holster. Could she actually use the knife on either Karl or Darren if she had to defend herself?

She pulled the door shut and shielded her eyes from the glare. The snow ran in huge drifts from west to east across the property. The actual porch wasn't too full of snow. The small pond where they'd landed was about two hundred metres away. She could get there without snowshoes—she hoped.

Lise struck out on an angle, trying to stay out of the deeper snow drifts and going back and forth in the easier ones. She didn't see any boot prints from the two men, so maybe they'd gone out the back door of the cabin. Why they'd leave without her and Rory to help them survive was a mystery. It was literal suicide.

Suddenly, animal tracks crossed diagonally against her path. She would've seen them sooner if she'd taken a direct route. Not polar bear tracks. The bears were all up on the shoreline of the Bay. These were wolf tracks, a pack of them traveling together. One set was larger than the others. They'd come through recently and since the storm ended.

She stopped and forced herself to look around three hundred and sixty degrees, turning on the spot to see if she could see any grey or white shapes traveling against the newly fallen snow. Wolves in a pack would be hunting and looking to make a fresh kill. She had no shotgun with cracker shells to ward them off, no regular gun to defend herself.

Dread clawed at the back of her throat. She almost turned to run back to the cabin, but the tracks were going away from her, so she fought against her panic and kept going to the helicopter. She quickened her pace and noticed how deadly quiet the early morning air had become.

The tracks picked up again on the frozen pond. The helicopter was shrouded in a huge drift of snow carved into jagged edges from the harsh wind. She could hardly tell where the door side was, and snow and ice completely engulfed the rotors. The downed aircraft looked like some bizarre art sculpture sticking up out of the tundra.

She noticed the wolf tracks went out and around the chopper, circling it, and a few of the more inquisitive animals had gone right up to the edges of the iced-over metal where it rested on the pond. Their exquisite sense of smell had picked up on the faint scent of the granola bars they'd carried. Would they be back? Not likely. They hadn't found anything worthwhile the first time. Still, she kept her head on a swivel, not wanting to turn around and find a pack of slavering wolves behind her.

Lise banged on the crust of ice where she remembered the side door being close to the ground. She swept away the crystallized snow and slammed her fist against the door latch several times. She pried at the door with Rory's knife blade, her breath pluming in the frigid air around her.

Radio. First Aid Kit. Was their shotgun still there? She'd been so focused on holding on to Rory's parka in the storm last night, she'd forgotten whether Karl still carried it with him. And could she get the motor started? How would she know if their ELT was working?

Idiot, she thought to herself. *You should've woken him up. You left him sleeping, defenseless. Some peace officer you are!*

She pounded the doorframe with both fists. *Stupid, stupid, stupid.* She had to get into it and get back to Rory. Tears of anger pricked her eyelids. She cursed herself all the way to Sunday.

The latch popped. With a sob, she dropped to her knees and pushed on the door until it opened to the side. She did a quick shoulder check for any wolves or other predators and then crawled into the sideways helicopter. She stashed the knife back in her right front pocket. The helicopter was off balance, but she still slid in far enough to find her portable radio caught between her old seat and the wall. She pressed the on switch.

"Churchill, it's Dumont. Churchill, come in, over."

She could hear faint static, but the light, which should've been green, didn't light up on the radio. She repeated her call.

"Churchill, JR one is down, JR one is down at Goose Lake."

Nothing. She clicked the button a few times and got nothing. Maybe she'd imagined the static. She thrust the radio into her front left pocket, anyway. The first aid kit had been on the floor in the back, but everything had slid around in their messy landing. She scrambled over the seat towards the front and slid her gloved hands along the floor to see if she could feel the square shape.

She was about to give up and crawl out backwards when her right hand hit the barrel of the shotgun. It was jammed way at the back and squeezed between the two broken seats. She lay on her stomach and pulled it forward as best as she could with her one hand.

Finally. Something was going her way. Even with just a cracker shell for defense, she could use the weapon against predators, whether animal or human. She bit her lip till it bled. The barrel moved a couple of inches forward and then got stuck on something. She rolled onto her left side and used her legs to brace herself. No way was she leaving without it.

She reached down with her left hand and used her legs as leverage when she pulled forward until the gun gave way. With a few heaves and pushes, she got it upright and free from the seats. She lay on her back, the gun across her chest, tasting her own blood in her mouth but with a silly grin on her face.

If only Aidan could see her now. Miles from civilization. No one knew where she was, and no one knew where to look for her. Sweat pouring off her and yet freezing at the same time. Clutching a shotgun and praying that wolves wouldn't smell her fear and double back, looking for a quick meal. Not exactly the society wife he'd been hoping for.

Lise gathered her strength and sat up. Her new perspective in the helicopter let her see the white corner of the first aid kit peeking out from behind the broken back seat. She squirmed over and yanked it up by its metal handle. Well, she'd accomplished two out of three goals for this little jaunt. Now, to get back to Rory and figure out what to do about the missing men.

She had an easier time getting out of the helicopter than

she had climbing in. She straightened up, checked the shotgun to make sure it was loaded, and wished she'd found the box of cracker shells. The one shot would have to make do. She carried the first aid kit under one arm and the shotgun over her dominant arm.

She stepped into her own tracks going back, so the walking was easier. The silence bothered her. Could the wolves be waiting behind the cabin or lurking in the short scrub brush nearby? Normally, they would hear the odd bird cry, even this far from town. She kept turning her head back and forth, just in case.

Still no sign of the convicts. She didn't bother to keep quiet. Better to let the wildlife know she was around. She banged up the short stairway onto the porch and shouldered her way into the cabin with the new gear.

"Hey, Rory, time to get up..." she said as she kicked snow from her boots and turned around with the shotgun at waist level.

"We beat you to it, darlin'." Darren smirked, his own shotgun at his shoulder and pointed at her head.

Rory sat in one of the easy chairs, his hands tied in front with plastic ties, his face translucent with pain.

Lise brought her own gun up to her shoulder, dropping the metal first aid kit to the floor with a loud clatter. Out of her peripheral vision, she saw Karl standing by the stove, holding a coffeepot in one hand.

"Guess we've got another of your Mexican standoffs," she said, sighting down the barrel. "Why're his hands tied up? He's injured. He's no threat to you."

"Gee, thanks," said Rory under his breath.

Darren shifted from foot to foot, his eyes squinting at her. She wanted to keep his attention focused on her in case Rory could get himself loose.

"No need for any shooting," said Karl. "I made coffee. Sort of, anyway."

"Shut up." Darren kept his eyes on Lise. "That's for your headache. You don't need to share."

"Put your gun down," said Lise.

"You first, sweetie," said Darren.

"For crying out loud, would the two of you knock it off?" Karl exclaimed, just before he keeled over in a dead faint, the coffeepot shattering on the floor.

Darren swung around to see what had happened, and Lise cracked him over the back of the head with her shotgun. He dropped to his knees, and she hit him again.

"Lise!" yelled Rory.

Darren fell over in a daze, and she landed beside him, quickly cuffing him with her handcuffs from her utility belt. Her shotgun landed by Rory's feet, and he used them to pull it towards him. She picked up Darren's shotgun and put it in Rory's lap. Then, she dove for Darren's front right pocket and retrieved her own gun. She shoved it back into its holster, then stepped over Darren's inert figure on the ground and headed over to Karl.

"Karl. Karl, can you hear me?" She slapped his face lightly on one cheek. "Wake up, please, please, wake up!" She put her cheek beside his lips to feel his breath. He was breathing, but barely. Putting two fingers on his carotid pulse, she waited until she got the faintest heartbeat.

"Is he dead?" Rory squirmed in his chair, trying to see what she was doing. "Did he faint, or did he stroke out?"

"He might've had a stroke," she muttered, checking his face with her fingertips. "His cheeks seem different. I've never seen someone go down like that without being hit."

Darren came to and started cursing at her, wiggling on the floor against the handcuffs.

"Keep it up, and they're going to tighten up on you," she said without looking at him. She kept shaking Karl's shoulders, then stopping to feel his pulse in his neck. "He's still breathing," she threw over her shoulder at Rory.

"We've got to get him back to Churchill," said Rory. "He needs a doctor and the Health Centre."

"I know, I know," Lise said. Panic sat on her shoulder. What would they do if he died? Darren would go crazy, even in handcuffs. By now, a search party should be out looking for them and the helicopter. "We need to get him back to town."

"How're you going to do that?" sneered Darren. "You going to teleport us out of here? You're as stupid as he is..."

"Just shut up," she said as she went through Karl's pockets. He had a wallet with some cash but no other weapons. Some plastic ties like cops used. His eyes fluttered, and she leaned over him, holding his face in her hands.

"Hey, you, glad to have you back with us, buddy!"

He made a few guttural noises in his throat and blinked a few times.

"Can you tell me your name?" she asked, one hand on his forehead. No fever, so he didn't have some hidden infection.

"Uh, my name... my name..." He broke off and looked at her with terror in his eyes. "What happened? Where am I?"

"You're at Goose Lake, near Churchill, near the arctic border." She sat back on her feet. "You fainted or something." She held up three fingers. "How many fingers do you see?"

"Three," he slurred. "I think, maybe."

Lise looked over her shoulder at Rory again. "He's concussed, or he's got a brain bleed. We need to figure out a way to let home know where we are..."

"Your radio work?" asked Rory.

"I put out a call, but the green light won't come on. I don't think anyone heard me."

"If they're looking for us at all, it'll be up north of town. Not down here," he said.

"This guy needs a doctor." She looked over at Darren. "We've got control now. We could make some kind of sled or travois and get them up to town."

Rory raised his hands into her line of vision, waving them to make her notice he was still cuffed with plastic ties. "Still got my knife?"

She jumped up from beside Karl and went over to the chair. "Here, sorry about that." She made quick work of the plastic.

Rory rubbed his reddened wrists. "Thanks. I say if the weather's clear, we try to follow the road up to town. When my brother-in-law Ben can't find us up north, he'll start circling out this way, and maybe the RCMP will spot us."

"What are we going to use to transport Karl?" She chewed on her lip as she stared at him on the floor. "He's conscious now, and hopefully, he stays that way. Darren can walk if I cuff him in the front."

"We're not going anywhere without our backpacks." Darren wiggled himself into a sitting position. "And I'm not carrying his for him."

"What's the deal with the backpacks?" Lise turned to Rory and whispered in his ear, "We should've searched those when we got in here last night."

"None of your freaking business." Darren's glare was pure acid.

"Yeah? I think it is my freaking business." Lise walked over to the over-stuffed chairs and pulled one of the black canvas bags over. She unzipped it, expecting to find clothes and maybe some food supplies. Or drugs. But it was filled with packs of $100 bills held together with a paper band around the middle.

"I thought you robbed a liquor store?" She pulled out

several packs in both hands. "How much is in here? Is the other one the same?"

"That's ours, and you can't touch it," snarled Darren. "It's money what was owed to us. Fair and square."

"I'll bet," said Rory. "I think it's evidence, and I'll bet my brother-in-law will be really interested in seeing it when we get into town."

"You take my money, and I'll kill you," said Darren.

"We'll take the money along with you and Karl and find help," said Lise. "First things first." She thrust the money back into the bag and zipped it up.

She put the two backpacks by the door and took the shotgun Darren had held away from Rory. Cracking it open, she checked the shot shells inside, then closed it back up.

"I'll be keeping this, and Rory will have the other one." She nodded to Darren. "Hold tight until we figure out how we're going to transport your cousin."

She pointed with her chin at the door and cocked her head at Rory. "Let's see what's outside and if there's anything in any other cabin we can use. Unless you think we can jerry-rig something with the mattress?"

Rory pulled himself up and hobbled over to the door. "That's our last resort. Let's see what else we can find."

He followed Lise onto the front porch, drawing on his fur gloves. The sunlight shone crisp and cold against the snow, making everything look like an icy, crystal paradise. He normally loved this time of year, even with an early blizzard. Looking at the snow against the porch of the cabin opposite to them, he estimated they'd had about twenty centimetres of snowfall.

He'd woken up to find both convicts standing over him and Lise gone in the early morning light. Darren had held the shotgun to his head while Karl pulled plastic ties from his pocket and secured him.

Even though he'd prayed for her safety, he had to admit, he was mighty glad to see Lise when she charged into the cabin again. Now they had the upper hand for the first time in over twenty-four hours, and he realized he was praying incoherent prayers that they could get at least to his cabin on the outskirts of town and his phone.

Lise circled around the back of the cabin. "Nothing back here," she yelled.

He staggered over to the one about ten feet away. The cabins were built close together on more of a walkway rather than a road. A couple of communal fire pits and laundry lines were in between the cabins. He sent up arrow prayers that they'd find something in this next cabin.

"Shouldn't you guard those two?" he asked as Lise joined him, her right hand on the handle of her handgun. He could tell she was more relaxed with her weapon back. "Not that I want to leave you alone with them..."

"Let's take a quick look," she said. "Unless Darren wants to walk himself up the road, he's not a threat at the moment."

They pried open the frozen doorknob after a few moments of pounding and using his knife blade. This cabin was the same layout, and Rory quickly skimmed over the bare furniture and contents.

"Aha!" He hobbled over to the threadbare couch. "Is this a sleeping bag?" He pulled at what looked like a blanket but turned out was indeed a dull green sleeping bag. It puffed up dust in the air as he hauled it off the couch, but otherwise, seemed to have no holes.

"What about your leg? You can't walk all the way to town

on it." Lise brushed aside the padded fabric and bent over to look at his thigh and the bloody towel wrapped around it. "You're going to start bleeding again."

"If I do, I do. I can't feel any blood right now." He manoeuvred the sleeping bag until he found the zipper and did it up. "We'll get there. If we stick to where the road should be, they'll see us more easily from the air when they come looking for us."

"What do you want to do with that?" she asked.

"We put Karl inside it, tie some of those laundry lines around him, and use them to drag him along the snow. It'll be uncomfortable and bumpy, but I don't see what else we can do."

"What about the mattress?" She lifted an eyebrow at the dusty green bag he was rolling up. "It's a bit cleaner."

"It's harder to manage if Darren gives us a hard time. We need to worry about Karl."

"You're right. Let's get back." She headed for the door.

"And Lise." He paused, feeling like a defective guy who should hand in his Man Card.

"Um?"

She turned, and the sun lit up her hair with a fiery halo. Her eyes sparkled, and she stood like an avenging angel in the doorway.

"You're going to have to pull him. I can help, but my shoulder... I..."

"We'll take turns. We'll be fine." She bounced back to him and planted a kiss full on his lips. Then she took the sleeping bag roll from him and headed down from the porch. "Let's go. It's going to take us a few hours, and I want everyone to eat something first."

She didn't look back. It was official. He was definitely in love.

CHAPTER 12

They made a strange-looking crew. Rory held the real shotgun leveled at Darren, who carried one clothesline attached to Karl's sleeping bag. Lise held the other one, and the two of them worked together to drag Karl with his head upright along the snow-covered road. Lise looked back at Rory as she hauled forward on the line. He was limping but keeping up.

She averted her eyes from Darren's endlessly running nose. For once, he wasn't complaining. His silence told her he might be plotting something, though. She kept one eye on him and one eye on Karl's face to check on him. So far, he was still conscious, but that might not last long.

"You alright?" she said to Rory.

"Fine." He grimaced but kept up his hobbling gait. She didn't see any fresh blood on the towel wrapped around his left thigh. "The cold is helping the pain."

She turned forward and matched Darren's longer steps. This was a new Darren. He kept his eyes on the horizon and his lips pressed together. Was he calculating what he'd do when they came in sight of the town? She knew he had no idea what their town looked like or where the docks were on Hudson Bay. They'd been planning on landing in Yellowknife in the opposite direction and would've studied maps for that area. They were over eleven hundred and seventy kilometres in the wrong direction. This idea of sailing to Europe through Hudson Bay was their last dying gasp of an escape plan.

Karl's breaths sounded laboured and shallow. They were all panting a bit in the cold. Still, the storm clouds had receded, and the sun blazed down on the winter landscape. The blizzard had dumped more snow than usual for their area, but at least the storm had only raged for twenty-four hours before blowing itself out.

The road from the cabins headed straight north and then west into Churchill. She calculated in her mind and figured they'd get there in about four hours if they kept up this pace. If they weren't dragging Karl, and Rory could walk quicker, they might have made it in over two hours.

Rory was right. She couldn't see any planes or helicopters overhead. They must be searching for them north of town, where they'd been going to relocate the polar bear. A rescue team wouldn't come south until they'd determined that Air One was nowhere to be found north of Churchill.

Some parts of their hike were less snowy, and short, scrubby trees popped up along the way. Lise kept her head on a swivel even though she knew, rationally, that polar bears were up by the Bay waiting for the ice to come in. They shouldn't see any bears down this way, but they couldn't afford to be caught off guard.

Darren was carrying his backpack, and they'd put the other one in the sleeping bag with Karl. She'd tied down the Conservation shotgun loaded with cracker shells on top of the sleeping bag, where she could grab it in case of an emergency. Like Darren pulling some kind of trick or a polar bear appearing out of nowhere.

"Why so quiet?" she asked Darren.

He glared at her, then hitched the clothesline up higher on his shoulder as he pulled his cousin. "What's there to talk about?"

"Do you need water? Another granola bar? We've got one left."

"Still trying to keep me alive so you can turn me over to the cops?"

She yanked on her own line as they maneuvered over some snowy lumps in the roadway. "Trying to keep you alive because I'm a decent human being."

He sneered at her. "Sure. Yeah. That uniform don't make you a decent human being. I've known lots of cops who were far from it."

"I'm not a cop, I'm a Conservation officer, and that makes me a peace officer." She glanced back at Karl, and then, satisfied he was still conscious, she said, "And I've known a few corrupt cops myself."

"Trying to make me like you ain't going to work," he said.

"Don't care if you like me. I'm curious why you keep blaming your cousin here for everything. Seems to me he's done a good job trying to take care of you most of your life."

Darren paused, staring at the ground as they trudged along. "He promised we'd get away this time. He's got *friends,* and I use that term loosely, who never come through for him." Darren sniffled.

"Sounds like he trusts the wrong people," said Lise.

"You can't trust nobody," Darren said as he shifted the clothesline riding on the strap of his backpack. "Ain't no one in this world you can trust but yourself."

"And yet, you two robbed a liquor store together," Lise prompted him, hoping he'd say more about it.

"They're easier than banks, have a ton of money in their

safes," he said, nodding as he spoke. "Karl does the planning and has this so-called crew working with him."

"Those friends," she said.

"Bunch of deadbeats. It was supposed to be him and two of his pals that night, only they didn't show up."

"Um hmm," she said.

"He calls me to meet him there, so I do. Says he's cased the place, and there's only two girls on before closing. In and out in five minutes kind of thing." He pulls harder on the sleeping bag, taking larger strides in his ill-fitting boots. "Turns out there's one girl and a manager who decides to be a hero and put up a fight. Had to shoot him. Wouldn't have gotten away otherwise."

"I see," said Lise. "What kind of fight did he put up?"

Darren snorted. "He decided at the last second to grab the money bag back and yelled at us he'd pushed the alarm. First time we'd heard about them being alarmed. Anyway, he's hanging on to the money bag, and he and Karl are going back and forth like a seesaw, so I shot him."

"And the poor girl?"

"She kept screaming, so I hit her over the head with the gun. She went down, too." He shrugged. "Karl grabbed the money bag, and we escaped." Darren spoke as though he was going to the grocery store to pick up a rotisserie chicken.

"And he died, so you guys are supposed to be doing twenty to life, right?" asked Lise. She shivered.

"The guy was stupid. The money belongs to the Liquor & Lotteries Commission. It's their money. Why would anyone risk their life for someone else's money?" he demanded. "Trying to show off in front of the girl and be a hero." He glared at Lise as if she didn't understand either. "No one needs to be a hero. That's for the movies. He should've let us go."

Lise digested his reasoning as they slogged along the road

with snow above their ankles. Dying for a bag of money didn't seem like a good enough reason to her, either, although she didn't enjoy thinking the same as a criminal.

"He was doing his job. He was the boss and keeping the store safe," she said.

"Like you were doing your job when we came across you guys?" He cocked an eyebrow at her. "I could've killed the both of you if I'd felt like it. You're lucky Karl didn't know how to fly a helicopter, or you'd both be dead right now."

She stopped in her tracks. "And lucky for you two, we knew some first aid, or Karl here would've died from this head injury. He may yet die. Have you even thought about that?"

Karl moaned as his head collided with her thigh. *Well, that's a good sign,* she thought. *He's definitely conscious.*

"Sorry, Karl," she said, lowering his head to the ground gently. "Let's take a quick break." She checked his eyes and put two fingers to his carotid pulse. "Keep hanging in there. We're more than halfway now."

Rory stood beside her; his breath frosted in the air. "I'll take a water bottle, please."

She dug one out of the plastic bags she'd tied to the crossed lines of the clothesline that kept everything on the sleeping bag. Karl wore her toque, and she'd put up her fur-lined hood on herself to keep out the cold.

Lise had wrapped him with all the sheets and blankets in the cabin, and then they'd rolled him into the sleeping bag. His nostrils and upper lip were frosted with ice from his breath.

"Karl, can you take a drink?" She proffered a water bottle to him. "You need to stay hydrated, too."

"Let's go, we're going to freeze to death standing around here." Darren had lost the whine, but he still grated on her last nerve.

Ignoring him, she held the bottle to Karl's lips and held the back of his head while he took a few sips.

Rory polished off half of his water and put the cap back on. The bottle disappeared into his parka pocket. "So, you do care about your cousin," he said to Darren. "Here," he said to Lise, "let me take the rope for a bit. You carry the gun." He handed her the shotgun and took the line from her.

She used her mitt to wipe away the water from Karl's chin so it wouldn't freeze on him. "Are you sure your shoulder can take it?"

"This is my good shoulder. Let's go." He hiked the plastic line over and nodded to Darren. "Try to keep up."

Darren snorted, and the two moved off so fast Karl yelped, "Hey!"

"Guys! This isn't a sprint. Let's make sure the poor man has some skin left on his back by the time we get there," she said.

She'd stopped in the middle of the so-called road to double-check the shotshells in the gun. Suddenly, from her left peripheral vision, she saw two sprinting grey wolves. She barely had time to react, shooting over their heads and yelling at the men to stop. The boom of the shotgun echoed across the open landscape, and the wolves ran wider and circled across the road from them, panting and running slowly back and forth.

"What do we do?" screamed Darren, who dropped the plastic line and grabbed onto Rory.

"Stand still and wave your arms," yelled Lise as she walked in front of the three men. "Wave your arms in the air, you two!"

She took aim to the left of the wolves and shot over their heads again. The crack and boom reverberated across the snow and made her ears ring for a few seconds. Darren and Rory were jumping up and down, waving their arms. She stood in front of Karl, feinted left and right, then turned backwards to see if more wolves were circling them.

"They look like they're alone," she said. "See, they're taking off now."

The wolves weren't exactly leaving. Their tongues lolling out of their mouths, they trotted away to a distance of about three hundred feet and then stood watching them.

"What's up with them?" asked Rory.

"They look older, and they're not with the pack I saw this morning," she said.

"You saw a wolf pack this morning and didn't bother to mention it?" He sounded angry, which she probably deserved, but worrying about Karl had been her primary concern.

"Only their tracks, not them exactly. They'd been out around the helicopter and then were coming northwest. These two seem to be separated, so maybe they're old or getting sick."

Darren stood swearing in the middle of the road, but staying within six inches of Rory, she noticed. His language was quite inventive.

"They must be starving to come at us like that," she said.

Karl had fainted again, but his pulse was steady. Maybe it was for the best. They could travel faster if he was unconscious unless Darren was too freaked out.

"I'm going to die up here, and no one will ever know!" screamed Darren. "I'm going to be torn apart by wild animals!"

"No one's going to die," said Lise. "This was a mated pair. An older pair, that's why we were able to scare them off." She put her mittened hands on his shoulders and gave him a shake. "We're almost there. Maybe another hour. You can do it."

"We should head to my place," said Rory. "It'll be shorter, and we can call for help for Karl without going right into town."

"You're right, but can you navigate us across without the road?" she asked.

"I've got a compass attachment to my watch." He pointed

to his wrist. "I never leave home without it. We can track straight west once we get to a certain landmark, I know."

"Okay then," she said. "That's what we'll do."

She was relieved to hand over some responsibility to him. Her heart was still pounding from seeing the wolves and shooting the older shotgun off. She handled all wildlife interactions, and she'd have to write a report when—she refused to say *if*—they got back to town.

Karl's breathing was even and shallow. She pulled part of the blanket up over his lower face and tucked it in around him the best she could.

"This is our last hike. Let's make it count." Rory handed Darren his part of the cord. "We keep moving, and we won't make ourselves as big a target."

CHAPTER 13

A stand of stunted coniferous trees came into sight amid some rolling snowdrifts. Rory's log cabin was off to the side of the trees. Despite the burning pain in his thigh and shoulder and his numbing exhaustion, he felt a surge of hope. Heat and food. He swore he hadn't seen Bosco in a year.

Lise shouted incoherently and jumped around, pumping the shotgun in the air in her hand. "We made it! Rory, we did it!"

She grabbed him by the arm and kissed his cheek as he and Darren stood wavering in the snow, still holding Karl's clotheslines over their shoulders.

"Wahoo!"

He laughed at her. She was definitely scaring away any wolves or other wildlife.

"Okay, let's get Karl inside. The heat should be on, and we can figure out next steps," he said. He cocked his head at Darren. "Let's get you warmed up, too."

"This your place? All the way out here?" Darren didn't move. "This is no better than where we were before."

"I guarantee my place has heat and food," said Rory. "Get a move on."

Darren sniffed but said nothing. They pulled Karl along quicker now that they were in sight of the cabin. Rory didn't mention his black truck parked around to the side. He wanted a chance to talk to Lise privately, if possible. And how to get their cell phones back?

They carried Karl between the three of them. The front door wasn't far, and Rory still had his keys in his parka pocket. The door opened to a welcome rush of heat, and Lise cried out in joy when it hit them in the face. They carried Karl into the living room and put him on the couch, still in the sleeping bag.

"We've got to call an ambulance. He needs to get to the Health Centre right away," Rory said, looking at Lise with a cocked eyebrow.

Would she remember Darren had their phones? Lise still carried the shotgun, but the other one was still resting on Karl's chest, tied down with clothesline. She should be in charge. She could get their phones back.

He needed her to understand. He slanted his head towards Darren and said, "Maybe we should call 911 right now?" His vision went blurry as he wavered on his feet. Exhaustion overwhelmed him, and he sank to the floor beside the couch.

"Rory!" Lise crouched beside him and put the shotgun down for a split second. "Are you bleeding again?"

Darren grabbed the shotgun and pointed it at her head. "No one's calling 911. Think I'm stupid? Think I don't know the cops will be out here and take us away?"

Rory cursed his weak body. He should be the one with the gun. He should be the one protecting Lise. *Why God? Why are You letting this happen to us?*

"Okay, okay," he ground out.

Lise had her hands out, ready to spring up. He saw her eyes were trained on Darren. The last thing he wanted was for her to get into a physical fight over the gun and one or both of them ending up shot in his living room.

"Listen, Darren, you can still get away from here," Rory said.

Darren waved the shotgun in his face. "Yeah? How's that?"

"You've taken us as hostages, right? And Lise is worth a lot as a peace officer—it's the same as a cop up here." He shot her a look of apology. "I parked my truck outside. It's full of gas. You take us as your hostages, and you've got leverage to get that boat you want. You get Karl checked out at the Health Centre, and you guys get on the boat, and you're out of here."

"What's this Health Centre you keep talking about?" Darren's eyes were slits of flinty blue, his hands rigid on the shotgun.

"It's our hospital up here. We just don't call it that," said Rory, shifting his bad shoulder. "There's an ER, and we can get Karl looked at by a proper doctor. You'll have us to get them to meet your demands. We'll all be in town." He stopped to catch his breath. "It's a win-win, man."

Lise edged upward on her knees. Rory prayed she didn't make a hero move on the gun.

"Listen to him, Darren. It's a great idea. Let's get Karl out to the truck now." She put her hands higher in the air to show surrender. "I'll even drive."

"No way, I don't trust you," said Darren. He waved the shotgun at Rory again. "He's the weaker of you. He can drive."

Karl groaned from the couch. "What are you doing now?" he croaked out.

"Never you mind," said Darren. "You two sit tight. I'm going to check this place out and see if you got anything worth re-selling." He laughed to himself and walked over to Rory's bookshelves. He scanned the glass and wood watch boxes.

"Well, well, looky here." He snorted. "I wouldn't have

pegged you for a jewelry guy." He started lifting the lids on the boxes.

"They're not jewelry; they're... *watches*. They're for different things."

"Yeah? Like telling time?" Darren chortled at his own joke. "How many watches does one guy need? You've got..." He started counting them one by one.

Rory suspected Darren wasn't too good at mental math.

"You've got fifty-two watches here. Man! That's a lot of jewellery for a backwoods lumberjack."

"Again, *not* jewellery. I *collect* watches. And there's no trees up here, so I'm not a lumberjack. Haven't you been paying attention to the terrain?"

"Terrain? What's that?" said Darren.

"For crying out loud," said Rory. He muttered something worse under his breath.

"Darren, we need to get Karl to a doctor," said Lise.

"Which ones are the most expensive?" said Darren. "Seems to me a guy who can buy fifty-two watches can afford to buy some with diamonds."

"Diamonds are for sissies," ground out Rory. "There's nothing there worth over ten grand."

Darren shot him a look of disbelief. "Then I guess you don't mind if I take a couple of boxes with me."

"Suit yourself." Rory pulled himself up from the floor and sat on the edge of the couch arm. "Go nuts. But we're taking Karl into town and getting him medical help."

He nodded to Lise, and she nodded she understood. He went to Karl's head, and she picked up his feet in the sleeping bag.

"Out the back door or the front?" she asked.

"The back door is quicker," he said, hefting Karl's head and shoulders up against his own chest. His bad shoulder screamed in agony as he did so. "Got him?"

"Got him," she said.

Out of the corner of his eye, he saw Darren take a watch box and try to shove it into his backpack of money. He couldn't tell which box, but they were all insured. His stomach clenched in anger at the thought of his irreplaceable watches, some from as far back as the Civil War, disappearing out the door with Darren.

Darren followed them outside as the two of them struggled to keep Karl up off the ground and get to the truck. He unlocked it with his keyless fob, and they put Karl down beside the truck. It rode high off the ground, but not as high as some guys drove their trucks in town.

He opened the back door wide. "Okay," he said to Darren. "You're going to help us get him in here, lying down. Then you can sit back here and keep an eye on us."

"No way. I'm sitting up front with you in case you try anything funny," said Darren.

"Let's get this over with," said Lise.

Rory could see a red flush flowing up her neck and cheeks. She was angry, and he had the fleeting thought that it was probably a good thing to separate the two of them.

The three of them worked to heave Karl up and into the back seat of the truck. Karl moaned and swore, so he was still conscious. That was a good sign. Rory jumped up into the driver's seat and adjusted his mirror so he could monitor Lise in the back.

Darren put his backpack at his feet and joined him in the front. He pointed the shotgun at Rory's face.

"Drive," was all he said.

❄

Lise crouched on the floor of the truck, one hand on Karl's chest to make sure he was still breathing. They'd come into town and onto Kelsey Boulevard, the main street. She peeked out the side window at the businesses and houses rolling by. The street was unnaturally quiet.

There were no trucks or snowmobiles outside of the RCMP detachment. She didn't see any snowmobiles outside of The Great Northern Lodge or Ruby's Café either. She prayed that meant that people were out looking for them and not that some other tragedy occurred during the blizzard.

She caught Rory's eye in the rear-view mirror and figured from the look on his face, he was thinking the same thing. They rolled down the main street and turned north on Ramsey to get up to the Health Centre, which was inside the Town Centre.

The Town Centre held everything they needed under one roof for safety. People could do their business, go bowling, go to the movies, the library, the daycare, or the hospital and see their doctor without worrying about driving around town and meeting up with polar bears.

She could still feel Karl's chest rising and falling, even though his eyes were now closed. Rory drove slowly along the newly plowed road and went around to the left of the building, coming in behind the ER doors. To their left was the ice-filled shore of Hudson Bay, the slushy water heading out to the horizon. To the right were the ER doors under the overhang, and she got ready to leave the truck.

"Hold on," commanded Darren, still pointing the shotgun straight at Rory's stomach. "Your girlfriend goes in to get a gurney for Karl. You stay put." He looked over his shoulder at Lise. "You say anything to anyone, alert the cops or an alarm, anything, and I shoot your hunk here. Got it?"

"Got it," she said. She nodded at Rory, trying to tell him with her eyes that she would follow his lead. She inhaled and blew out one breath, then pushed open the truck door and jumped out. "I'll be right back."

Lise headed straight for the ER doors. She had no doubt in her mind that Darren meant what he said. He had nothing to lose at this point. He'd made it clear he wasn't going back to jail. Rory was her only concern.

Lise shook the snow off her boots inside and scanned the hallway leading to the waiting room. Children cried, and a high shriek filled the air. The ER was busy for mid-afternoon on a Monday. She strode up the hallway, hands in her pockets, trying to look nonchalant but glancing up once at the security camera on the ceiling.

She hooked a left into the ER proper and stood to the side, sizing up the people and staff. Every chair in the waiting room seemed to hold a sick child. Her stomach flipped looking at them all. Two nurses sped up and down the beds in the ER, but she didn't see either Mike or Colin, the orderlies.

What she wouldn't give for a couple of male bodies. She sidled over to the counter and tried to peek at a computer underneath the overhang shelf. All she saw were names and coloured boxes. No schedule appeared to be posted anywhere on the walls. She prayed Joy Koper wasn't on today.

Another nurse appeared out of nowhere, dashing to grab the ringing phone. The woman answered with a cocked an eyebrow at Lise as if to say, "What?"

Lise smiled and waved her off, turning around and heading out to the other side of the hallway. The X-Ray department was down that way, along with Security and the elevators upstairs to the Maternity ward. She spotted a couple of gurneys by the wall outside of X-Ray and grabbed one.

Several women in scrubs passed her, staring at their phones or clipboards, as Lise pushed the gurney down the hall. She got to the Security office door, but the doorknob was locked.

Should she slip a note under the door? Lise dug around in her pockets but didn't have paper or pen.

Frustrated, she headed out to the truck with the gurney. She didn't want Darren to go off half-cocked and figured she and Rory could come up with a plan once they got inside. The high number of children present worried her. Darren was too desperate to care about collateral damage.

The automatic doors opened for the gurney. Wind swept into the area between the two sets of doors and billowed around her open parka. She prayed an ambulance would drive up or someone else would come to the doors from the parking lot, but no one appeared.

Darren leaped from the truck and slammed the door. "It's 'bout time. I was about to come in myself." He waved the shotgun openly at her. "Get over here now."

She rolled the gurney up to him and couldn't resist shoving it into his legs. She still had her service weapon. This wasn't a lost cause. Plans flipped through her mind like a highlight reel. Someone might spot them from one of the hospital windows and see Darren with the shotgun. Surely, someone inside would call 911.

"Karl!" he called as he opened the back door of the truck.

Rory appeared around the back bumper, bent over and grasping his leg wound. She registered his pallor and the sweat on his face as Darren put the shotgun on the roof of the truck. He leaned in to get his cousin to sit up.

Lise grabbed the shotgun awkwardly from the roof. Darren dove around the open back door for it, and then they both held it between them. Up close, his breath and stink nearly overcame her as they wrestled chest to chest.

"Lise!" she could hear Rory yell from what seemed to be far away.

No way was she letting go of the shotgun. Darren tried to

trip her, but she was lighter and danced sideways, drawing him with her. Around and around they went, until his weight pushed them onto the snowbank the plow had made in the parking lot. She held on to the gun even when he took one of his hands off and smashed it over her nose and eyes.

"Lise, Lise," Rory yelled.

Why isn't he coming to help me?

Darren started pawing at her right side for her service weapon, and she threw herself onto that side to keep him away. They rolled together in the snow, and Darren went over top of her for a brief second. The force of his fall was enough to break his hold, and she pulled the shotgun back toward her.

"Stop! Stop right freaking now or so help me, I'll shoot!" she yelled. She clambered to her knees with the shotgun at her waist, aiming it right at Darren's head where he sat in the snowbank.

His eyes rolled, showing their whites like a wild horse, and he threw his hands in the air. "Come and get me!" he shrieked at the bystanders. "She's going to kill me! She's crazy. She's going to kill me!"

Lise panted hard as she staggered to her feet. "On your stomach. Now!"

He took one look at her face and flopped over onto his stomach. Lise could see people crowding in the ER doorway now, with Rory hanging on to the side of the gurney. He waved at her and then took a swan dive onto the parking lot.

That broke the spell. She jumped on Darren and handcuffed him. Two orderlies ran to Rory from the door and picked him up and put him on the gurney. She had no idea what happened to him or what was wrong with him. Her heart thrummed in her chest, and blood pounded in her ears. For a second, she thought she would pass out, too.

"Are you going to take me in where it's warm or what?"

Darren shivered uncontrollably beneath her. She realized she was holding his head down on the snow.

"Rory," was all she could croak out. Tears came, and her nose started running as a nurse clutching her sweater around herself sidled up to her.

"You okay? Do you need someone to help bring him in?" said the woman.

"Security, please," Lise said, wiping her tears and trying to look professional.

"I'm soaking wet down here," Darren whined.

"Shut up," she said, pushing his head back down. "You're under arrest."

CHAPTER 14

Lise stood back and let the new nurse who'd helped her outside cut off Rory's makeshift bandage. Darren sat handcuffed on a gurney across from them in the opposite ER bay, along with a pimply-faced security guard.

"Who's the doctor on today?" she asked, keeping one eye on Darren as he sat shivering under a blanket. They'd taken away his outdoor jacket because it was soaking wet.

"Dr. Stedman. He'll be down in a minute." The nurse peeled back the bloody towel wrapped around Rory's leg. She expertly made two cuts in the jean material and opened it.

A horrific stench filled the air, and Lise put her hand up to her mouth. Rory's thigh was bright red, with two striations coming from the biggest slash mark. His upper leg was swollen, and the two wounds oozed with a green, odious discharge.

"Oh, no!" Lise grabbed the side handrail of the gurney. "There was nothing to wash them with out there. This is all my fault."

"He's got a fever, and we need to get an IV into him right away," said the nurse, whose name tag read Amy. "I need some help over here!"

Two girls came running. They calmly shoved her to one

side, and the bigger of the two whipped out a plastic IV kit, and the other hung up a saline bag. Lise stumbled backwards. Everyone moved at lightning speed.

A doctor appeared at her elbow. "You brought him in?" he said.

Lise nodded. "I need to call his mother."

"I won't know if he's in imminent danger till we get some blood work done. It could be a Staphylococcus A infection, and we don't want that, do we?"

"No, no, we don't... is Constable Ben Koper on duty? Are any of the RCMP guys around?" she asked.

"They're all out looking for the two escapees," he said over his shoulder as he put on his stethoscope and leaned over Rory's chest.

"I've got them both here. I need to call Ben," she said to the doctor's back.

She stood in the centre of the ER hall, not knowing which way to turn. The doctor continued to ignore her as he ordered blood tests and a tray of instruments to clean out Rory's wounds.

Lise turned back to Darren. When she'd handcuffed him to the gurney he was seated on, she'd taken back their cell phones, along with his wallet, ID, and the knife he'd used to attack Rory.

She'd stuffed their cell phones in her front parka pocket and got a paper bag from the bedside table to put the knife in. Rory's blood was still visible on it. Her training was wildlife, but she watched enough TV cop shows to know evidence that had been wet didn't go into plastic bags.

She had accompanied Karl to X-ray for a CT scan of his head and handcuffed him to that gurney as well. Her head pounded with the weight of responsibility for the two convicts.

Lise took up Darren's sodden jacket from the one chair in

the bay and searched the pockets again in case she'd missed something. Nothing. She yanked on the handcuff chain that attached Darren to the handrail to make sure it was secure.

"When's the doc going to check me out?" His whine was back.

"There's nothing wrong with you." She was past patience with him. "Not even frostbite, which is amazing considering those oversized boots you're wearing."

"How d'you know?" he sneered. "Can't feel my feet. Can't feel my hands neither."

"I'm so done with you." She pulled on the chain one more time. "Sit still, don't say a word. I'll be right back."

Lise rolled her eyes at the boyish security guard standing against the wall. He smiled and gave her a thumbs-up signal.

Three gurney bays lined each side of the room, and they were all full, including Rory and Darren. She walked over to the circular counter at the end of the room and pulled out her cell phone. Only one bar left, enough to call the admin number for the RCMP detachment. She didn't want to call 911 and start an emergency when everything was under control so far.

"Trudy Devlin. Churchill RCMP."

"Trudy, it's Lise Dumont. I need to speak to Ben Koper right away."

"Lise! Where are you? Everyone's out looking for you and Rory."

"We're in the ER. And I've got both of the escapees, too. One's got a severe head injury and is getting a CT scan, and the other one may be hypothermic or whatever. He's waiting to be seen."

"Oh, thank goodness! Ben's up with John McIsaac flying a grid search for you guys up to Arviat. We figured you'd gone down in the blizzard when you took that bear up north."

"No, it's a long story, but I need one officer over here.

Rory's in terrible shape, and I want to call his mom and tell her. I have to turn these guys over to the RCMP before anything else happens."

"I'll radio and let them know, but Zack and Adam are out on snowmobiles looking for you guys, too. And I think Scott and Braden are also searching with a whack of volunteers."

"Are you saying there's no one around?" said Lise.

"Not in town right now. I'll radio them right away. Can you hold on to both guys?"

"Yeah, one is trouble, but the other convict has a head injury, like I said. He'll probably be admitted. But Ben needs to know right away," said Lise.

"Gotcha. I'll call you back and tell you what Ben says," said Trudy.

Lise hung up and rolled her aching shoulders and neck. She really needed backup, and the sooner, the better. Uncontrollable shaking started in her legs and flowed upward over her body. She clutched at the counter to keep upright and steady.

"You okay?" said an older nurse as she walked in and wiped her hands with antibacterial gel.

"It's my adrenaline," said Lise. "I think I'm going to throw up."

The woman was at her shoulder so fast, Lise swore she didn't see her move. The nurse put her arm around her shoulders and brought her around the counter.

"Sit down here and put your head down for a minute." She gently put Lise on a plastic chair. "There you go. It'll wear off. Do you want water?"

Lise nodded, her head swimming and her body still shaking. She snaked out a foot to bring the garbage pail closer, just in case. The nurse brought her a paper cup of water.

"Sip it slowly. Are you sure you're not injured anywhere? Any frostbite?"

The older woman's kind eyes reminded Lise of her gramma's dark brown ones. She patted Lise on the shoulder reassuringly.

"Is there anything I should tell Dr. Stedman about you, hon?"

"No, really, I'm fine. It's Rory... Rory Gallagher we need to be worried about," said Lise.

Well, this proved she'd never make a cop if ever she'd thought of switching careers. She did much better with wild animals than with wild men, apparently.

The nurse laid her fingers on Lise's left wrist and counted off her pulse, then said, "I think we'll take your blood pressure and oxygen just for the record." She popped a thermometer in Lise's mouth and briskly wrapped a blood pressure cuff around her arm. It tightened to an unbearable squeezing pain, then eased off.

"I told you, I'm fine," she said, as Karl rolled by on the gurney, swung around by a female aide she didn't know. Was Kira Tanner the only one still in town who knew her from before? Workers could be transient in the north, but she used to pop in here and have coffee with several female friends.

"How is he?" She stood too fast, and the nurse pressed her on the shoulder to sit down again. "Don't remove those cuffs until the RCMP tells you to," she called out to the girl with the stretcher.

"We can't tell you his medical status, hon, because of privacy laws, but I can tell you he'll be admitted for that head injury."

Another nurse handed Lise the phone, the long cord snaking around her shoulders. "It's for you."

"Hello?" said Lise.

"Trudy here. Ben says they'll be there in an hour, so hold tight. They're ecstatic to hear you guys are okay."

"Thanks, although Rory is definitely *not* okay. Is Joy or Ruby coming over? Because I should call Ruby and tell her what's happened to him."

"He said he'd call Ruby. You stay with Rory and those prisoners till he gets there with reinforcements. You'll be up for some kind of medal for this, girlfriend. Talk about an adventure in your first week back!"

Lise laughed ruefully. "Some kind of medal, yeah. All I want is to stay with Rory, so the sooner the guys get here, the better."

"Call me if you need anything else," said Trudy. She hung up.

Lise gave the phone back to the young woman typing into the computer on the desk. She headed over to the end of the hall where the vending machines sat. Her stomach was nauseous from not eating anything. She wondered how long it would be before they had Rory's injury under control.

She pounded on the vending machine till it dropped two chocolate bars and a bag of chips. The next machine held hot drinks, so she bought herself a double double coffee, even though she knew it would taste like hot burnt wood.

She jumped like a cat on fire when she turned around and Dr. Stedman was standing behind her.

"Sorry, Rory's asking for you. He's been in and out of consciousness with his fever. It's good you brought him in when you did."

"He drove us here," Lise said, shoving the chocolate bars into her front pocket. "I can't believe I didn't realize how bad off he was getting. I'm so sorry."

"Don't beat yourself up. He's known for his, shall we say, lack of loquaciousness?" The doctor smiled and patted her shoulder. "I imagine all he cared about was getting you here safely."

"I'll go sit with him then," she said. "I'm sure his mom and sister will be here any moment."

"I've checked on your other prisoner, and he's fine, by the way. No frostbite and no broken ribs or sign of concussion."

Lise gave an unladylike snort. "That one has nine lives, like a cat. Thanks, doctor."

"My pleasure. I've got two women about to give birth upstairs, so I'll pop back later to check in on Rory." He headed off to the elevators.

Lise made double-time over to Rory's sick bay. She put her coffee on the tiny bedside table beside his gurney and dumped their cell phones into the top drawer. His eyes were closed, and his auburn eyelashes were slashes of bright colour against his pallid skin. She buried her fingers in those spiky red curls on top of his head and brushed some of them from his forehead. His skin burned to the touch.

She checked his IV bag and the line going into his hand. The nurses had stripped his clothes from him and put him into a hospital gown, with his left leg propped up on a pillow. His thigh was re-bandaged properly with gauze and padding, and the stink was gone.

She glanced over her shoulder before she moved the sheet further away from his leg to check on the swelling. The thigh was still red, but those two obvious lines trailing from the knife slashes seemed to be fainter. Or was it her imagination? A nurse came to the foot of the stretcher, and Lise tugged the sheet back in place.

"We're pumping him full of antibiotics and a mild painkiller. He didn't want any painkiller, but Dr. Stedman persuaded him he needed to get some sleep. Hopefully, we caught the infection in time. It might've been a much different outcome."

"Different how?" she asked.

"If you guys hadn't gotten in here when you did, he could've gone septic. He still might."

"Thank you." Lise's throat closed up.

He'd been so stoic and never complained of the pain or showed how incapacitated he had been. She couldn't believe what he'd suffered and not let on. The nurse moved away, and Lise pulled the solitary chair over to the side of the gurney. She took Rory's hand in hers and rubbed the back with her thumb.

"I'm so sorry. You should've told me," she whispered. "You could've died from a staph infection." She leaned over the handrail and gripped his hand with both of her hands. Tears fell, and she turned her head to the wall so no one could see her cry.

"I've never known anyone like you." She kissed his hand. "I'm so glad it was you with me on that bear relocation."

"Does this mean we're friends?" Rory's eyes stayed closed, but his words slurred.

She gasped and stood up over the gurney. "I'd say a life and death experience is definitely the making of a beautiful friendship. How do you feel?"

He licked his chapped lips, his eyes still closed. "Like I want to cut my entire leg off. The doc says as long as the pain doesn't go past my groin, that's a good thing."

"Do you want some water? I'll get you some water." She released his hand and charged over to the nurse's station. "Where can I find water for a patient?" she asked.

"In the break room." The young woman pointed down the hall towards the x-ray section.

Lise sprinted down that way and grabbed a small beaker and plastic glass. She filled the beaker with tap water and headed back to Rory's gurney. He'd opened his eyes and gave her a half-grin when she poured out the water.

"Here, take small sips," she said as she held the glass to his lips. "Do you want some ice chips? Anything else?"

He shook his head, closing his eyes again. "This medicine's making me tired."

She pulled open the one drawer on the bedside table and found a facecloth and a kidney basin. "I'm going to wet this cloth and be right back." She was back in less than a minute and put the cloth on his forehead. "My mom used to do this when we had fevers. It'll help cool you down," she said.

"So hot," he murmured.

"I know. You're going to be okay. Darren and Karl are under control. Ben will be here in an hour."

"Why so long?" he asked.

Lise glanced across the ER and saw Darren lying flat on his stretcher, covered in blankets. She couldn't tell if he was awake or asleep.

She repositioned the washcloth on Rory's forehead and made sure his pulsometer was on his index finger properly. Exhaustion was overcoming her. She'd love nothing more than to find a spare bed somewhere and curl up and sleep for at least twelve hours.

"You were right. The cops flew north looking for us. Everyone else is out on snowmobiles doing a grid search." She kissed his hand again. "We can hold on. Everything will be all right."

She stared into the warm amber of his eyes as he smiled up at her. They crinkled elfishly when he lifted his left eyebrow at her. The noises of the ER faded away as she leaned over him.

"You're so beautiful," he said. "Your hair looks like a Rembrandt painting."

"I think that's the painkiller talking." She laughed. "My hair's a mess, and I need a shower, bad."

"No, no painkiller," he said, pulling on her hand. "Come here."

She didn't resist his kiss. Her mouth slanted over his perfectly, and her gratitude that they'd both survived their ordeal brought fresh tears to her eyes. His right hand slid around the back of her neck to deepen the kiss, and his lips moved over hers, searching and teasing until she was breathless.

When he pressed his lips to hers in one last caress, a shiver of sensation cascaded through her chest and arms.

"More than friends," he said, as they pulled apart slightly. Her tears fell on his cheek, and he wiped them away with his left index finger.

"More than friends," she agreed, pressing her forehead to his and then kissing it.

"I'm not exactly a spectacular date," he said. "Pretty boring."

She burst out laughing, then put her head down on his good shoulder to muffle her near hysterical laughter. "So boring! I don't know if I can take much more of this kind of boredom."

He tried to encircle her with his good arm but only managed to pat her awkwardly on the back. "I have a favour to ask."

"Anything." She lifted her head and sat on the plastic chair beside the gurney.

"Feed Bosco for me?"

"Of course. Where are your keys?" she asked.

"No idea. Where's my stuff?" He still held her hand tight.

"Your clothes are right here. Things were flying everywhere when you first came in." She pulled his parka from the enormous plastic bag they'd thrown all his clothes in beside the bed. His keys were in the left pocket, and she shoved them in her front jeans pocket.

"His food's in a bag beside the fridge. He gets some wet canned and some dry kibble."

"I think I can manage," she said, giggling. *What is wrong with me?* "Sorry, it's just that Bosco seems like such a tiny thing to be worried about after the past forty-eight hours. I think I'm punchy from all the adrenaline leaving my body."

A nurse came alongside the gurney opposite to her, checking the IV line, and putting the blood pressure cuff on Rory's arm. "I have to take his vitals, and I'll be out of your hair." She looked up and screamed, a piercing scream that lifted the hair on Lise's arms.

The woman stared right past her. Lise turned around to see Darren standing in the middle of the room, holding the security guard with his forearm across the guy's neck, a scalpel at his throat.

How did he get out of the cuffs? Where did he get a scalpel?

Darren yanked the young guard tighter across the throat with his forearm and waved the scalpel at Lise. "Shut up!" he screamed at the nurse, who was still howling.

Terror swept across the guard's face, and he mumbled something unintelligible.

"Shut up!" Darren shook the young guy hard. "You." He pointed the scalpel at Lise. "Give me your gun. Now."

Lise stood slowly, ignoring Rory, who was trying to sit up. She put out her hands in an entreating gesture. "Let's not do anything stupid, Darren," she said. "You've already got kidnapping for us. This will only make it worse."

"Give. Me. Your. Gun." He snorted back phlegm and spit on the floor. The scalpel went back to the guard's throat, and he moaned.

"You want my gun? Take me instead of him," said Lise. "That's fair."

"Lise, no," said Rory. "Wait for Ben."

She turned away from Rory so she could concentrate on the situation in front of her. "That's the deal. You can have my gun, but you have to let him go and take me with you." She put her hand on the butt of her Sig Sauer. "See? I know what you want. I can take you to the boats."

He licked his lips.

"Let him go."

Time telescoped around her like before. Blood pounded in her ears, and her vision narrowed until all she saw was Darren and his trembling hand holding the scalpel to the guard's pale throat. Close up.

She put out her hand towards them. "Me for him, and you can have my gun."

"No tricks," he said.

"You have my word." Lise walked towards the two of them, the staff, and patients in her peripheral vision like actors on a stage. "Come on. You know my word is good." She removed her gun from its holster and held out her left hand at the same time. "Come here, buddy. It's okay," she said.

"Lise, please wait," said Rory from far away.

Darren shoved the guard towards her, and she grabbed his arm and pushed him with her left arm behind her.

Darren seized her, turned her around, and held the scalpel to her throat. "Yeah, I know you," he said. "Can't trust you for a second."

"Here's my gun," she said, handing it to him backwards, butt end first. "Now what, tough guy?"

He grabbed it away from her and dropped the scalpel on the floor. He put the gun to her forehead.

"Now we take your boyfriend's truck, and you find me a boat."

CHAPTER 15

Rory lay back on the gurney, waves of dizziness flowing over him. The nurse beside him crumpled to her knees, sobbing, while others ran around in confusion. He closed his eyes against the bright light as nausea clawed its way up his throat.

The sight of Lise putting her parka on and marching out ahead of Darren had sapped him. Her straight back, her hair a fiery mass of curls, and Darren pushing her along at gunpoint—the thought of her out there with that madman made him vomit over the far side of the stretcher.

Horrible spasms wracked his body. Someone was yelling incoherently for anyone to call 911. People were shrieking. He wiped his mouth with the sheet and clung to the handrail.

God protect her. Give her the right words to calm him down. Where is Ben? Why aren't you ending this?

If ever God needed to show up, now was the time.

"Prove to me You're real!" he shouted.

"Are you alright?" asked an orderly who appeared at his bedside. "Who's real?"

Rory waved him off with one hand, his forehead on the handrail.

"Let's get you cleaned up," said the older man. He pulled off the soiled top sheet and handed Rory a pack of wet wipes. "If you can manage, I'll be back with a new top for you."

Rory lay back on his pillows. He shivered even though the room was hot. His leg still pulsed with fiery pain, but so far, it was all in his knee and thigh. That was good. He figured the nausea was from fear and adrenaline.

The orderly came back with a clean hospital gown and motioned for him to sit up. "Here you go," he said. "I've got to clean up the floor. Do you want a heated blanket?"

"I want my cell phone," said Rory.

The man yanked open the bedside table drawer and rifled through whatever was inside. He came up with a black cell phone and a blue one and held them up to Rory with a questioning look.

"The blue one," Rory ground out. "Thank you." The orderly headed off, probably to find a mop. He called the RCMP admin number and got Trudy.

"Churchill RCMP." She sounded breathless.

"Trudy, where's Ben? When's he getting over to the ER? Catcheway's taken Lise hostage, and they're heading down to the docks."

"Yeah, I've gotten about twenty calls on it, and I've reached Ben... just a sec." She turned away from the phone, and he heard muffled voices. "Hang on, I thought that was Zeke and Adam coming in, but it was Braden from the Conservation office."

"Radio everyone and tell them to get down to the docks. She's unarmed, and he has her service weapon."

"What's the male's description?" she asked.

"It's Darren Catcheway, and he's wearing black khaki pants, a hospital gown, and his blue ski jacket. No hat. Oversize boots."

"Got it," she said. "I'll get it out on the radio. Rory, they'll get there."

"I'm not betting on it," he said. "Does Braden have a vehicle?"

"Yes, a snowmobile."

"Send him over to the ER to get me," he said. "I'll be ready."

"Lise said you were in horrible shape. Rory, don't do anything stupid."

"He's going to kill her. Send Braden." He hung up.

Children were crying, but from where he lay, he couldn't see the security guard Darren had snatched. The rush of people had gone, and the nurses were clustered around their workstation, speaking in whispers to each other.

He peeled the tape off the IV in his hand, wincing at the ridiculous amount of pain the glue raised on his skin. Pulling the actual IV needle out was much worse, but he told himself to suck it up and tossed the IV needle to the side. He wrestled with the handrail until he got it to lower and swung his legs over the bed. No one was paying any attention to him.

Rory was glad Lise had pulled out the plastic bag containing his clothes. They'd ruined his jeans, but he didn't care. He had plain cotton hospital pants on and jammed his sock feet into his boots. Then he yanked his long-sleeve T-shirt out and ground his teeth as he got that on over his aching shoulder. His plaid flannel shirt buttoned up, he grabbed his parka and put it on.

The IV painkiller made him woozy, but he got his hat and mitts on. He stumbled to the ER door and into the hallway, then turned right to go out to the parking lot. His cell phone was in his hand to call Braden, but a snowmobile came screaming to a halt outside the enormous glass doors.

Rory hobbled forward and waved at Braden. At least, he

thought the driver was Braden. He didn't care. He was commandeering this snowmobile, regardless.

"Here's a helmet," said the figure in a one-piece snowmobile suit.

Rory accepted the black helmet and took off his hat, shoving it in his front pocket. Helmet on, he slid onto the seat and grabbed the handlebars at the rear. He rapped his fist on the back of the driver, and the guy gunned the machine, turning in a wide swathe away from the doors and heading down the parking lot.

"Ben's only fifteen minutes away at most," said the voice in his ear.

He wasn't used to hearing anyone in his own snowmobile helmet, but this confirmed he was with Braden.

"They'll meet us down there," echoed the voice. "Sit tight!"

He clung to the handlebars on the rear and sat forward slightly to distribute his weight. They shot off and headed south down to Kelsey Boulevard. Braden barely stopped at the stop sign and turned west to go out to the docks area.

"Are you sure that he's taking her down here?"

"He thinks he can escape in a boat to Europe," yelled Rory. "Sorry, she made a point of saying they'd go to the docks, so that's where she'll steer him," he said in a normal tone, realizing he didn't need to yell into the microphone.

"We should be there in two minutes," said Braden as they raced along the road, far exceeding the speed limit.

The snowmobile went airborne over low snowdrifts beside the roadway, landing hard and then shooting forward as it maintained its speed. Rory's body slammed back down onto the seat several times, his tailbone sending seismic jolts of pain up his spine. The landscape blurred beside his peripheral vision into a white haze.

Braden slowed enough to corner into the parking lot for the

city docks. Rory swayed side to side on the back of the snowmobile, his gorge rising at the back of his throat. They screamed down the incline to the dock area filled with two trailers, now locked up for winter. The snow-filled lot had been plowed out. In summertime, it was beaten down sand and gravel.

A huge, matted guard dog came running at them, barking and showing its teeth, but Rory didn't even flinch. The steps down to the cement dock were covered in snow and ice, but water inside this narrowed area of the Churchill River crested around the rocks leading away from the long dock that ran horizontally to the shore.

Rory jumped off the back of the snowmobile, stumbling for a couple of steps as he yanked off the helmet. A red-hulled touring boat was plowing through the waters and away from them toward the enormous mouth of the river.

Darren still obviously thought his plan to head to Europe would work. Their boat was headed out into the harsh waters of Hudson Bay from the river. Rory cupped his eyes with his hands to see better.

Two figures were in the boat, and it was running at high speed. Even from this distance, he recognized Lise's flamboyant red hair.

"Tell Ben to follow me," he commanded Braden.

Rory charged down the snowy steps to the main dock. Several boats were still tied up at the wooden docks attached at right angles to the permanent cement one. They should have been lifted out this weekend. For now, he was thankful they were still at hand.

They ranged from rowboat-size to a larger fishing boat. If Darren insisted on heading out onto the Bay, Rory needed the bigger boat to give chase. A man Rory didn't recognize was wiping down the inside of the fishing boat. He untied the huge rope from the metal cleat and threw the rope into the boat.

"What are you doing?" Braden yelled at him. "Wait for the cops."

"He'll kill her and throw her overboard," Rory yelled back. He jumped onto the boat, sliding a bit into the snowy slush on the floor. His heart beat a tattoo against his chest, and his knees buckled. He grabbed the steering wheel in terror.

Now was not the time for a panic attack, and yet the rocking of the boat in the current splashing against the dock was restricting his breathing. Literal dots floated in front of his eyes. He'd always thought that was a cliché in books. He shook his head to clear his vision, but they wouldn't go away.

"What're you doing, man?" said the guy in surprise.

"I need your boat," Rory ground out. "I need to catch that boat out there." He pointed towards the other boat with the red hull, which was doing a slow turn and going in a northerly direction.

"Hey, you're bleeding, buddy," said the boat owner. "I'm calling the cops."

"The cops are coming! You need to give me the boat, or follow that boat," panted Rory. "Please, do it! You'll be saving her life."

"I don't want no part of this, man," said the guy, backing up with his hands in the air.

"Fine. Get off. I'll do it myself." Rory shoved past the man and turned over the key in the ignition. "Get off, I said."

The guy clambered over the side onto the dock and made wild gestures at Braden.

"Rory, stop," yelled Braden. "Wait for the cops."

Rory gunned the motor and put the boat in reverse to move away from the dock. Then he shoved the throttle ahead to put the boat into forward drive, aiming it at the other boat now going in wide circles. He couldn't tell what the people were doing in the other boat, or if they were even still on it.

Please, God. Please, don't let her be dead. Don't let her be dead. I'll do anything, anything, just let her be alive... let her be alive.

He suddenly realized he was riding up and down on waves, cutting across the river, back on the water again. The other half of his mind grasped he had no weapon other than a paddle to take out Darren if he got the chance.

He squinted his eyes to focus in on the red-hulled boat going around for another wide circle. He was almost upon them. Where was Lise?

Lise's nose was bleeding, and her eye was going to swell closed, but her fingers dug deep into Darren's side muscles, and she threw a leg over his in a pincer move to keep him down. Rory's knife lay buried in her front pocket. She knew she had one last chance to get her gun back from him before he killed her and dumped her body overboard.

Their grunts and moans shot into the air as each of them struggled to grab the Sig Sauer. Darren punched her twice, hitting her shoulder and the side of her head. She saw stars for a few seconds but didn't lose her grip on him. Adrenaline coursed through her arms, and she grabbed him by the hair and pounded his head into the floor of the boat.

You fight like a girl. She could hear her cousin mocking her when they were eight and nine years old. *You're a dirty fighter.*

Well, dirty fighting was going to keep her alive. She bit down on his ear hard. He shrieked, but the bite loosened his grip enough that she yanked the gun back, rolling onto her back and then away from him.

She scrambled to her knees, pointing the gun at him two-handed. "Stop!"

"You skanky…" Darren roared, pushing off the floor and coming at her.

She aimed the gun. Pulled the trigger. Darren fell back against the floor, holding his upper leg and screaming to high heaven. Blood flowed between his fingers, and she knew she'd probably hit the femoral artery.

"Lise!" She heard Rory's voice from far away, but Rory wasn't here. He was in the hospital. She'd seen him lying on the gurney, clutching the handrail, when Darren shoved her gun into her temple.

It was just she and Darren, alone out here on the water, going in circles because Darren put the boat on auto before he'd tried to shoot her.

"Lise! Pull me in." Sounded like Rory again, except she was shaking; her legs and arms trembled like leaves on a breeze. She was so, so cold. Everything was freezing out here. She stood over Darren, pointing the gun at his head, shaking and shaking.

The boat crested a high wave, and it threw her sideways, still holding on to the gun with an iron grip. She was never letting go of her weapon again, not for a thousand security guards. The boat rose again, and she slid down the side of the boat, pointing the gun at Darren between her legs as he screeched like a rabbit in a steel trap.

"Lise, come on. It's me. You're okay, sweetheart. It's okay."

Her head bounced off the wall, making her realize how much she ached all over. Her nose started bleeding again, and she wiped it with her hand. She kept the gun pointed at Darren but used her left arm to pull herself up to a standing position.

"Darren, you're lucky I'm not in that boat." Rory stood on a boat beside theirs, and she finally realized he was really there. He was doubled over the side of the boat, holding his hand out to her. How was he out here?

"Hang on, Lise. Help's coming."

Blood from her forehead trickled down her cheek. Her right eye was puffing up, and the right side of her head clanged like choir bells.

"What are you doing here?" she said. Stupid. Everything seemed telescoped far away. Except Darren. His screams were scraping the inside of her brain. She turned from Rory and pointed the gun at Darren. *Keep holding it two-handed*, she told herself.

Vaguely, she heard Rory talking to someone else. She hardened her stance against the waves and maintained her position. *I almost died. He almost killed me.* Her thoughts were flitting around her head like the arctic terns flying around them overhead.

"Lise, the RCMP is on their way. They're coming in their boat. Sweetheart, can you look at me?"

She shook her head, concentrating on Darren's face. It was scrunched up in terror and pain. Tears and snot ran down his cheeks. He clutched his thigh with both hands, but his blood still pooled on the boat floor in the slush.

"I'm going to die out here," he shrieked. She heard that clearly.

"You were going to kill me," she whispered.

"Lise, you need to put a tourniquet on him." She heard Rory's voice again.

Lise had her back to the voice. Was he still here? Was he in the hospital? She couldn't tell anymore. Her head hurt so bad, like a thousand hammers were pounding on her, and she couldn't see out of it.

"Lise! I'm not kidding. He's going to bleed out. Tie something around his leg."

"Lady, please," Darren whimpered now.

You don't have to fight anymore, she heard in her mind. *He's my child, too. Fix him.*

Like fog lifting from her eyes, she realized Rory was right. Darren's white face and hands were dangerous signs of blood loss, not to mention how much was already on the floor of the boat. She put her gun back into her holster and braced herself with her hands on the edge of the boat.

She scanned the area for something to use as a tourniquet. The two front seats and a back bench were empty. She stepped over Darren's inert body and flipped open the back bench. A roll of yellow marine rope lay inside, so she grabbed it and knelt in the muck beside Darren. She wrapped the rope twice around his thigh above the bullet hole and tied it off. A tape measure lay by the side of the seat, so she used that as a brace for the knot to hold it tight.

Darren released his hold and flopped back onto the floor. She didn't care if he'd fainted or not as long as the bleeding was under control. Another boat appeared alongside them. She realized they were still moving in a circle, although slowly enough that Rory and the RCMP boat could keep up with her.

"I've got this," she yelled over to Ben in the RCMP boat. She waved at the two cops and went to the front of her boat and cut the power. The boat came to a stop, wallowing in the waves from side to side. She kept her hand on the butt of her gun.

The RCMP boat came closer, and Ben pulled the two boats together by hand. "You alright?" he asked.

"Does she look all right?" said Rory. "Of course, she's not all right."

Lise held up one hand. "I just want to get back to land. Can someone take this guy?"

"Adam's going to hold our boat steady, and then I'll come on board and take him off your hands." Ben climbed aboard and helped her pull Darren into a sitting position. At least he was awake and hadn't lost consciousness.

"You're under arrest for kidnapping, assault, assault on a

peace officer, and escape custody," said Ben. "I'll read you your rights when we get to land." He hauled Darren's arms behind him and handcuffed him. "If you hold your gun on him, I'll drive the boat back to the mainland. Or do you want to drive the boat?" Ben asked her.

"You drive," she said. "I'm pretty woozy." She took her gun out and pointed it at Darren sitting sideways on the other front seat. "Not that woozy that I won't shoot you again."

Darren hung his head to his chest. His shoulders and muscles shrunk into his body.

Lise nodded at Ben. "Let's go home."

Ben waved at Rory on the boat beside them. She cast a quick look Rory's way, wondering what he thought of her battered face. It began to dawn on her that he was *here in person,* not in the hospital where he was supposed to be getting IV treatment for his staph infection.

He'd come out onto the river, where he'd sworn he'd never go again. To follow her. To save her, help her. She stared at his back as he drove his boat in front of them across the choppy waves towards shore.

He'd faced down his fear and come after her. He'd sacrificed for her. No one had ever done that for her before. As they bumped up and over the waves, she kept her gun trained on Darren and prayed that she would never be involved in a manhunt again.

CHAPTER 16

Rory refused any treatment until Lise had her CT scan, and they admitted her for observation. By then, Joy had entered his room to wrangle him into submission. She carried an IV kit and another hospital gown.

"She's coming back here, although it's not protocol to put a male and female together in the same room," she said to him as she hung up the saline bag. The smaller bag containing his antibiotics was already hanging on the metal stand. "Put this on, and I'll be right back to put in your IV."

"Thanks for this," he said. He scowled as he sat on the side of the bed, his left shoulder and infected leg screaming in pain.

She stopped at the door. "Can you manage? I can help you."

He waved her off. "I'm okay. Everything hurts. When's my next painkiller?"

Joy laughed. "You can have it after supper, hero. If anyone deserves a painkiller it's you."

He nodded as he rubbed his bad shoulder. "I'm not so heroic I'd go without it."

"I'll be right back," said Joy.

Rory pulled on the hospital gown and managed to tie it in

the back. He'd gotten new cotton pants, and Joy gave him two sets of acrylic hospital socks, but his feet were still blocks of ice.

He was in a semi-private room overlooking the parking lot. They promised the other bed to Lise. She had a concussion and was downstairs getting stitches in her forehead. He wished he was the one getting them. She didn't strike him as being vain, but no woman wanted a scar on her face.

Joy brought in another blanket. "Will you get into bed? I scooped this from the warming oven." She bustled around, getting him tucked in and the guardrail up on his bed. She took up the IV tubing and needle from the bedside table and told him to make a fist. "Okay, let's see your veins," she said, tapping on the back of his hand.

"Can you use this one? I've already got a bruise on my left hand from the first IV," he complained.

"That's the least of your worries," she said, as she found a vein. "Take a deep breath now, in and out." She inserted the needle as he took in a breath and slid it all the way in.

"You're good at that. It didn't hurt at all." He sighed as she taped the needle down with a square insert of plastic. "The other nurse in the ER just about skewered my entire hand."

Joy fussed with his sheet and blanket. "Let me check that thigh now. And don't be shy. I want to make sure the new dressing is secure and see how red your skin is..."

"Sis." He grabbed her hand to make her stop moving. "Enough. I'm good. The doc said the antibiotics will take my fever down."

Tears glistened in her eyes, and her mouth trembled. "Rory, we thought you were gone..." She put the back of her hand against her lips and turned away from him, her shoulders shaking.

"I'm going to be fine," he said. "Don't cry. Mom did enough

crying for both of you." He reached for her, but she walked over to the other bed and sat.

"First, they can't find your helicopter, then I hear from Trudy you're badly injured. Next thing I know, you've eloped from the ER..."

"Eloped? Doesn't that mean running away to get married?" He laughed, even though it hurt every muscle in his body. "I haven't had time to ask her."

"No, you idiot. It also means a patient who leaves the hospital while under treatment. No one knew where you'd gone until Ben radioed into town that you were out there *in a boat*." She spit out the words like they were a euphemism for something despicable.

"Speaking of boats, why weren't those boats lifted out last weekend? I was surprised there was no icy slush up against the shore from the blizzard."

"You know the river water's always a few degrees warmer down at the docks," Joy said, wiping her tears. "I can't believe we almost lost you. Just like Dad."

"I wasn't thinking of that. All I was thinking was getting to Lise," he said.

"Yeah, you weren't thinking at all. Ben was on his way."

"You don't know this Darren guy like I do." He stared up at the ceiling. "I knew he would kill her as soon as he figured out how to run the boat. He would've thrown her overboard."

"Ben and the guys still got there in time." She crossed her arms and tossed her chin the way he knew from childhood. She wasn't going to lose this argument. To her, her husband was invincible and on the same par as a superhero.

"And it was good they did because Ben arrested him, and he didn't die. Lise isn't going to face questions about how or why she shot him." He shifted on the bed to get comfortable. "Lise is lucky to be alive."

"You're lucky to be alive with that infection. You're going to be in here for at least a week." She stood and wiped her nose with a tissue from the bedside table. "Get some rest. Supper's soon, and I'll check in on you later." She kissed him on the top of his head. "Very glad we didn't lose you, bro." She ruffled his dirty, spikey curls.

"Hey," he protested. "I'm not hungry. How about that painkiller?"

"Eat something," she commanded. "Anything."

Lise and her orderly appeared in the doorway. He steered her in with her wheelchair to the side of the other bed.

Her forehead sported a broad, white stick-on bandage, and her chin had two small butterfly strips on a cut. Her right eye was swollen to a slit, and the surrounding area was a charming maroon.

"Can't see out of this eye." She pointed to it. "This my bed?"

"Yes, do you need help getting settled?" asked Joy.

"I'm good," she said.

Lise wore normal clothes, Rory noticed with some irritation. Where were her hospital gown and hospital slippers? She carried a navy-blue plastic bag he recognized from his mother's Café and Emporium.

"Hey," he said to her as she put the bag on her bedside table. *Well, that was suave.* He couldn't think of something intelligent to say after all they'd been through. He watched her climb onto the bed, clutching the plastic bag to her chest.

"Why don't you slide under the covers? Supper will be here shortly," said Joy.

"Sure." Lise lay back and put her left hand over her forehead. "Not sure I can eat anything. This headache's pretty bad."

"I've ordered you soup and crackers with some gelatin.

Only fluids for now with that concussion," said Joy. She glanced at Lise's file the orderly had left on the over-the-bed table. "Looks like you're going to be our guest here for at least forty-eight hours."

Rory caught her worried look as she stared at Lise, who kept her eyes covered.

"Do you want the curtains shut? The lights off? We can move you to another room if that would help."

He thought Lise moaned but couldn't be sure. He tried to sit up, but his bossy sister put her hand up in a "stop" gesture, even as she kept her stare on Lise. She walked up to Lise's bedside.

"I know my brother wants you right here where he can keep an eye on you, but you are able to choose for yourself if you want a private room," she said quietly. "I'll still be your nurse. That concussion is nothing to fool around with, Lise."

"I... thank you. Just hurts, that's all. I want to stay here."

"All right. Your call button is right here." Joy moved Lise's hand to touch the white metal button on a cord she'd wrapped around the guardrail, so she knew where it was, and then patted her hand. "Call me for any reason."

"Yes," whispered Lise.

"You two get some rest. If you're sleeping, I'll leave your supper trays on your bed tables at the end here." She motioned to the rolling tables at the end of the beds.

"Thanks, sis," Rory said with emotion. He figured his mom would be back with her Café food, so he wasn't worried about eating hospital food, but he'd make sure Lise stuck to her liquid diet.

Joy finally left after fussing again with his blanket. Everything hurt, like he'd told her, but he managed to turn his head to the right enough to see Lise. Had she fallen asleep, or was she passed out? Her hand had dropped from her face and rested on her lap. She must be all right because he could see the even rise and fall of her chest.

He scrunched down in his blankets and did his best to turn onto his right side, dragging his swollen left leg on top. Agony and stabbing pain were his reward, but he could put up with that to watch Lise sleep.

Rest, sweetheart. You're safe now. I'm not going anywhere.

Lise vaguely remembered trying some chicken soup last night and Joy checking on her vitals in the darkened room several times. The curtains were closed, and the outside was still black, but her empty stomach told her breakfast time would be soon. Her head ached with a reverberating pain she'd never experienced before. Her eyes burned and throbbed.

Concussion protocol. The doctor had given her instructions, but she didn't remember those at all. When Darren first clocked her head against the edge of the boat, she'd nearly blacked out but held on out of sheer guts. All she'd cared about was getting her gun away from him and not dying out on the water.

Now, she might have damage from a severe concussion. She knew from playing girls' rugby in high school that her injury was serious. Still, that was nothing compared to Rory having organ failure if his infection spread.

Guilt choked her, and she muffled a sob as she lay on her side, away from Rory. Why hadn't she thought about washing out the wounds better? Why hadn't she noticed how much he was struggling? She'd been out of her depth. She wasn't a cop. She was used to dealing with animals—the four-legged kind with fur and claws—not the two-legged kind who posed far more danger.

For a few minutes, she gave herself over to self-pity. Hot tears fell onto her pillow, and she covered her nose and mouth so Rory couldn't hear her cry. She was lost. And alone. The looks the nurses shot between them when they checked Rory's leg yesterday showed their incredulity at how badly she'd field-dressed the wound.

Crying made her head hurt more. She bit her lip and forced herself to take a deep breath. She wouldn't be able to stand the pain if it got much worse. And the nurse wouldn't be by with their medications until breakfast time.

She rolled over slowly so as not to wake Rory and reached for the box of tissues on her bedside table. Wiping her eyes and nose, she nestled into her pillow and pulled up the thin blanket. Sleep was gone. At least she felt back to normal in the appetite department. Where was her watch? Her cell phone? She was bereft without her belongings.

A bag from Ruby's Café and Emporium sat on the chair. A hand-written card from Ruby sat on her bedside table. *"I hope you'll enjoy these new clothes on the house. Anything else I can do, call me. Love, Ruby."* She pulled the blanket up to her chin and stared around the room, jumping when she met with Rory's cat-like amber eyes staring at her from across the four feet between their beds.

His smile widened as she jerked in surprise.

"Good morning." His voice was rough. "You slept right through."

"How do you know? How did you sleep?"

"I got a few winks," he said, his right arm crossed under his chin. "I was worried about you being asleep with that concussion, even though Joy told me it was all right. That must be an old wives' tale about getting woken up every hour."

"I do remember her taking my vitals during the night," she whispered. "I think."

"She did," he whispered back. "I guess that's how she knew you were okay."

"How's the leg?" she asked.

"Sore," he said. He quirked an eyebrow at her.

"Just sore?" she said.

He shrugged. "I feel like roadkill."

She gave a harsh laugh. "I look like roadkill."

"You look beautiful to me," he said earnestly.

She was lost for words. The intimacy of being in a dark room, even though they were in hospital beds four feet apart, felt more profound than when they'd lain together for warmth and survival on the bed in the cabin.

"You owe me a story," she said. She couldn't think of anything brilliant to say.

"Yeah? How's that?"

"You told me you'd tell me how you were adopted," she said. In the dim light, she doubted he could see her blushing, but she wanted to get the attention off herself.

He huffed out a laugh. "You have the memory of an elephant. I'm impressed."

"Speaking of having an excellent memory, Joy sent Jake to feed Bosco last night."

"Jake Miller from The Great Northern Lodge?" Rory asked.

"Yeah, he showed up along with Lukas Tanner to see how you were doing, and Joy took your keys from me and sent them off to feed Bosco and check on your place." Lise's chest relaxed, and she put her palm under her cheek against the pillow. "She told them you couldn't have visitors for at least twenty-four hours."

"That's my sister, bossing everyone around," he said, but he said it with admiration. "I'm surprised mom didn't show up with food for everyone."

"She took food over to the RCMP office after she left you," said Lise.

Rory lifted his head off the pillow. "You're kidding me!"

"She wanted to thank the volunteers who were looking for us, so she and two girls from the Café fed everyone." Lise smiled. "I really love your mom. I want to be her when I grow up."

"Hey, girl," he said, reaching across the void between their beds. "You *are* her already. I've never seen a woman fight a man like you fought with Darren. And that's not just once; that's twice you took him down."

Lise snorted. "Yeah, the thought of dying will do that for you." She held his hand and squeezed it, then let it go. "Now, tell me how you were adopted."

He laughed again. "You do have a one-track mind." He rolled onto his back. "Someone left me on the steps of St. Mary's Roman Catholic Church here on a spring night in May. I've been told that Father Mike was closing up when he heard what he thought was a dog whining outside. It didn't stop, and the noise disturbed him, so he opened the main door to chase it away." He stopped for a few seconds, staring at the ceiling in the shadowy light. "And there I was, wrapped in a couple of flannel blankets, wearing a disposable diaper, and lying in a plastic dishpan."

"You're kidding!" Lise sat up so abruptly that she made herself woozy. "A dishpan... oh, Rory... I don't know what to say."

"Hey, it could've been a fish bucket." He laughed. "Apparently, I started squalling as soon as he picked up the plastic bowl. Ruby and Rob Gallagher were walking with one of their foster kids, and Ruby rushed over to see what was going on."

Lise propped herself up on her elbow to watch him. "I

thought stories of babies being left on church steps were urban legends."

"Ruby examined me and saw someone had tied my umbilical cord off right, so someone knew what they were doing. She insisted they take me to the Health Centre to be checked out."

He lay in silence, staring at the ceiling. The silence filled the crevasses of the room, and Lise held her breath until he spoke again.

"Father Mike baptized me because I was underweight and not as responsive as the doctor would've liked. Ruby and Rob came to visit me every day in the nursery. She fed me and sang Cree lullabies to me."

"In a town this small... surely, they found your real mom?" As soon as she asked the question, she regretted it. How painful to realize his own mother had left him outside, on the steps, not even inside the warm church building.

Rory huffed and tried to roll toward her, but she saw the physical pain etched on his face.

"You don't have to tell me any more," she said.

"The RCMP went door to door, asking every family in town if they knew anything about the abandoned baby. Not to mention my flaming red hair that was an anomaly in this town." He twisted his face as he pulled his left leg on top of his right with both hands. "They had a few ideas, but this was thirty-four years ago. DNA testing wasn't a thing, and no parents were letting on that their daughter had just given birth."

"So, how did you end up with Ruby and Rob?" she asked.

"They were already foster parents and in the CFS system. They volunteered to bring me home from the nursery once the doctor cleared me. And they adopted me formally when I was nearly two, once CFS exhausted every potential lead to see if I had birth parents anywhere."

"They must have been amazing parents," she said.

"They were... I hit the lottery. If they hadn't come forward, I would've been flown south and ended up in foster care in Winnipeg. They gave me a genuine family, and I'll do anything for Ruby and Joy."

"Your dad," she started to say.

"Rob." He paused for a long time. Again, she was afraid to break the silence. "He loved all of those little girls they fostered over the years—I have no idea why they never ended up with a boy—but he certainly showed me how to hunt and fish and appreciate their culture."

"Did anyone in town have red hair back then? It's a recessive gene, but you must've wondered as you grew up." She couldn't resist the obvious question.

"I asked Father Mike once. He served here until he got cancer about four years ago. He told me he couldn't break the seal of the confessional. So, he eventually knew who my birth mother was but couldn't tell me. And I didn't care. I was happy with Ruby and Rob."

"So, they baptized you Catholic," she said.

"Yeah, but I was raised at Grace Community Church. Ruby made sure we went to Sunday School and confirmation class." He sounded amused. "Dad and I preferred our trapping and fishing trips to spending Sunday mornings at church."

"Sounds like Father Mike did the right thing, not telling you the truth." She paused and sighed. "Sometimes the truth really does hurt."

He smiled at her. "Joy is a busybody, and she went to the high school after she came back here as a nurse and looked at the old yearbooks going back thirty-five years. There was a male teacher up here then who taught phys ed and what they called "shop." He had flaming red hair. And he mysteriously left in the winter of 1988 without even resigning. Jumped on the train and disappeared."

"So, you think your birth mom was a high school student?"

"Probably. And if my gene donor was that coward, I was thrilled to have Rob for my adoptive father." He shook his head. "I just couldn't save him."

"You did everything you could, Rory. Just like you saved me," she said.

"I think we saved each other, sweetheart."

"If it weren't for my poor first aid skills, you wouldn't have that infection," she said.

The door opened, and an aide came in with a tray of food. She put it down on Lise's table. "This is for you, my dear." She turned to Rory. "You're on clear fluids until we get that fever down."

She flung open the curtains, and Lise covered her eyes with her hands. The light was grey and pallid but still hurt her eyes. The aide brought in another tray smelling of weak tea and consommé.

A nurse in neon pink scrubs bustled in behind her and popped a thermometer into Rory's mouth. "Time for your vitals. Let's see how you're doing since 4:00 a.m. this morning." She wrapped the blood pressure cuff around his bicep and let it pump up.

Lise tried to sit up and then gave up the effort. She pushed the button on the inside of her bedrail to lift her high enough. With the wash of morning light, she could see how pale Rory's face was against his fierce red hair. His red stubble slashed across his chin and cheekbones because he hadn't shaved in days.

"Your temp is up another degree," announced the nurse. "You need sleep. If you two are going to keep yakking, I'm going to get the charge nurse to put you in different rooms. I don't care what your big sister says." She glared at Rory before exiting the room.

"I didn't think we talked that loud," said Lise.

Rory made a feeble effort to grasp his mug of tea. "Maybe they thought my adoption story was riveting. I know school kids used to make a lot of fun of me being a 'changeling' back in the day."

Lise pulled the over-the-bed table towards herself. It held a bowl of watery oatmeal, a mug of weak coffee, and a bowl of cut-up fruit. Her stomach growled despite her massive headache.

"Try to drink that up," she said. "And I won't bother you for stories anymore."

When she looked over, he was sound asleep.

CHAPTER 17

Rory floated over the snowy tundra. The air shone crisp and clear around him, but he felt no cold. He put his face up to the sun but didn't feel its warmth either. Beneath him, he spotted a lone wolf padding along on the crusty snow. Bent, stunted trees hung over with ice that glistened in the light.

Why couldn't he feel his feet? He was vibrant and full of energy. The massive wolf trotted along before him as if on a mission. He could see every spike of its rough fur, every individual colour in its coat. The majestic wolf pulled him along in its orbit, and he followed the animal with no effort on his part.

"It's spreading. He's going septic. We need to upgrade the antibiotics." The voice in his head was loud. Was it in his head?

"He's in danger of getting endocarditis," said another voice. Why was he hearing strange voices in his head?

"Why is his body reacting this way? He's an active, healthy, thirty-four-year-old man." That was his sister, Joy. Bossy as usual.

"He never should have been out on the water. Who let him get out of the ER?" said the second voice. He sounded angry. Why were they arguing?

Rory didn't feel any pain. He couldn't feel his legs or his feet, but at least he didn't feel any pain. He stayed right on track with the wolf, which went up to a crack in the ice-covered stream and begin to drink.

"You have to save my son's life."

Mom? What are you doing in my dream? thought Rory. The wolf turned its head to look at him, its yellow eyes kind and knowing. *He understands me. He reminds me of someone.*

"You flew me all the way up here. Why'd you bother if you're not going to listen to me?" said the second male voice. "He's going to die."

"I wanted a second opinion. I say we try heroic measures."

"You can try, but that boat trip likely killed him. You need to prepare the family," said the second male voice.

"Please, just save my son."

Mom? What's going on?

Rory watched the wolf leave the stream without looking back. It traveled straight out into the snowy, vast tundra. He watched it until it disappeared from his sight. Then everything went black.

Wednesday, November 2
1:00 a.m.

The lights were dim in the ICU department, and Lise spied Rory immediately in the centre bay as she entered through the massive doors. Two nurses glided around on rubber soles, checking the other two patients on the ward. Lise's chest unclenched when she realized Rory was getting one-on-one attention.

Ruby got up and hugged her in a bone-crunching hug from the chair beside Rory's bed.

"What are you doing here, my girl? You should be sleeping for that concussion," Ruby said.

"Can't sleep. I wanted to bring you a coffee, even though it's not much." Lise handed her a latte she made at her place with the fancy coffeemaker she got as a wedding shower gift. She glanced at the bed.

"Only one visitor at a time," said the nurse in melon scrubs with yellow flowers. She stared at Lise with a baleful eye, arms akimbo. "It's the middle of the night."

"It's fine," said Ruby. "I'm going to take a break and enjoy this delicious coffee." She patted Lise on the shoulder and gestured to the chair. "I'm sure he'll sense that you're here. It'll be good for him. Healing."

The nurse frowned but said, "A brief visit."

"How is he?" asked Lise, fear stamped on her face. Her stomach did backflips, and she was glad she didn't bother bringing a coffee for herself. Her throat closed up, and she was shocked by the ashen pallor of Rory's face against the sheets of his hospital bed.

"He's fighting for his life," said the nurse. "He's got a thirty percent chance of recovery. He was in peak health before the infection, so he's got that going for him."

Lise nodded and licked her chapped lips as the nurse walked back to the circular desk in the middle of the room. Lise pulled the chair over to the bed and picked up his left hand. Her tears fell hot and fast on his hand, and she muffled her sobs against his skin.

"Oh, dear God, heal him. He doesn't deserve this, and I don't want him to suffer for my mistake. Please heal him and bring him back to me. I'd give anything to do it over again. Please bring him back to me."

She rose to kiss his forehead and brushed back his hair one more time. His skin was burning hot with the raging fever.

"That's a good prayer. Prayer always helps," said Ruby. "I know God is looking out for my boy." She stood at the end of the bed.

"Ruby, I'm so, so sorry," gulped Lise. "I'd do anything to change places with him."

"Hush, now! That's the last thing he'd want, and you know it." She smiled at Lise. "Besides, I'm sure you two have got quite a bond after everything you've been through."

"I never even thanked him for the flowers." Lise wiped at her eyes. "I meant to when we were flying the bear up north, but then..."

Ruby smiled at her and sipped her coffee. "You can thank him when he wakes up, my girl."

"What do the doctors say?"

"They've given him broad-spectrum antibiotics for the sepsis. Much higher grade than penicillin. We have to keep praying and wait and see." She rearranged the blanket over Rory's feet, her hands expertly smoothing out the wrinkles. "He's in God's hands."

"He's not going to lose his leg, is he?" asked Lise.

Ruby hesitated. "No. They're worried about his heart. We're praying for a complete healing."

Lise burst into tears, ugly crying, her hands over her mouth to stifle her sobs. She plunked down in the chair and rocked back and forth in agony. Ruby got down on her knees and hugged her tight. She let Lise cry on her shoulder, muffling her weeping so the nurse didn't come over. She let Lise cry herself out and then offered her a tissue from her jeans pocket.

"Here now, my girl, this one's pretty clean."

Lise couldn't speak. How could his mother be so kind to her after everything that happened? She didn't deserve it. Lise only wanted to see him open his eyes. Those beautiful, amber-brown eyes that crinkled at the edges when he laughed at her.

"You've been through so much the past few days. You have to get better yourself."

Lise's head hurt on a scale way beyond ten. Her concussion would take a few months to resolve—Dr. Stedman had told her that when he discharged her earlier in the day. He'd printed out concussion protocols for her and given her a note for time off work. She didn't care. All she cared about was Rory waking up.

"I want to stay with him. Thank you for being so understanding," she said.

"Shh," said Ruby. "I'm going to sneak another chair in here. If we sit against the wall, I don't think they'll complain too much."

Ruby watched the nurse at the desk until she disappeared into the other sick bay and then tiptoed towards the closed door going to the hallway. The ridge of light under the door shone obliquely on the floor. She picked up a padded chair like it was nothing and brought it back to Rory's bedside.

Lise thought of her own mother's angry texts on her phone since their story hit the news yesterday. Why her mother was angry with her was a mystery. She contrasted the tone of the texts with Ruby's gracious hand squeeze as she sat beside her.

"Keep your parka around your shoulders. It gets chilly in here when you're sitting still. You'd think they'd keep it warmer for the patients, but the nurse said not when they're trying to deal with fevers," said Ruby.

Lise obediently pulled up her fur-lined hood and brought her parka around her shoulders. She settled into the chair and crossed her arms, her head against the wall. Before she knew what happened, she fell sound asleep.

❄

Friday, November 4
9:00 a.m.

Rory opened his eyes to see Ben Koper standing beside his bed. The tall cop towered over him and blocked the light overhead in his ICU bay.

"You're not the one I wanted to see," croaked Rory. The words stuck in his parched throat. His body lay heavy on the hospital bed, and his headache throbbed dully behind his eyes.

"No doubt, but I popped in to check on you," said Ben. "The nurse said your fever's gone down to almost normal."

"Yeah?"

"Can I get you anything?" asked Ben.

"Drink of water," said Rory, pressing his lips together. His leg wasn't raw with pain, just aching at a dull roar. Almost manageable.

Ben offered him a straw in a glass of ice water. The big man's hands were gentle and kind as they maneuvered the straw into position.

Rory gulped the water gratefully. It flowed down his throat like a balm. Sleep crusted his eyes, and he knew his breath would stink. No more sensations of weightlessness.

"What day is it?" he asked.

"Friday. You've been out of it for about seventy-two hours. Mom and Lise have been keeping you company," said Ben.

"Lise..." said Rory.

"She's fine. We got her statement on your ordeal, and we can wait on yours."

Rory closed his eyes for a few seconds. "Darren and Karl." The effort to speak was like running down a street at full tilt. His heart thrummed in his chest.

"Relax, buddy. We don't want you stressing yourself," said Ben.

"No, we don't, and I'm going to have to ask you to leave if his vitals change any more than they have," said the ICU nurse, who appeared at the end of the bed.

Ben turned to show her the RCMP flash on his parka, and she sniffed in disdain.

"I don't care if you are the police. He's barely woken up and needs to be kept quiet."

"Yes, ma'am," said Ben, coughing to hide his amusement. "Just visiting my brother-in-law."

She turned away in a huff.

"What happened to... them?" asked Rory.

"Darren's back in Thompson, securely in jail, and waiting for his new trial. He's got additional charges of escape custody, kidnapping, and assault police. Karl, unfortunately, didn't make it," said Ben.

"What?"

"He had a brain bleed. A slow one, but it finally took him the day before yesterday," said Ben.

Rory looked at him in disbelief. "Does Lise know? She did everything to keep that guy alive."

"She knows." Ben nodded. "He had it from the time of the plane crash, and even if he'd come right in and had surgery, his odds were only seventy-thirty, the doc said."

"She'll be upset," said Rory. "Where is she?"

"Resting at home on your mother's orders. She was actually in here with you all night," said Ben.

"Oh."

"When you're all better and home again, we'll take your statement. Meantime, all you have to worry about is recovering." Ben patted him on his shoulder. "You've got a lovely lady to go home to." He gave Rory a big grin. "At least you got something out of this mess."

Rory took a couple of deep breaths after Ben walked out.

Did he have Lise? He'd been in blackness, or sleep, other than his weird dream where he heard voices. And saw that wolf on the tundra.

You've got a lovely lady to go home to.
I'm praying you're right, Ben.

CHAPTER 18

Thursday, November 10
Churchill, Manitoba

Lise ushered her mother and Aidan to their reserved table at The Great Northern Lodge. They sat beside one of the picture windows, looking out over the rear of the property, where the snow-filled tundra spread out to the horizon. Her mother plunked down on her chair and dusted away an imaginary speck of dust from her plate setting.

Aidan sat opposite to Lise, his back to the window. She knew he didn't care about the beauty that lay outside. He preferred to watch the people who filled the restaurant for dinner, his one eyebrow crooked so far up his forehead she thought it might disappear. His disdain for the wine list was obvious, and he put down the plasticized menu with an eye roll.

"I'm glad you finally agreed to meet with us," he said to her.

His greenish hazel eyes behind sandy eyelashes seemed weak to her now. His suit was an immaculate cut of tailored wool in a deep grey, his tie Italian silk in maroon. Sizing him up over her menu, she estimated the ensemble cost him at least five thousand dollars. And his 18-carat gold pinky ring with the ruby probably a lot more.

Her mother, meanwhile, had definitely splurged on her own clothes for this dual ambush campaign up north. She wore a floral designer dress Lise knew she couldn't possibly afford on a bookkeeper's salary. Aidan likely bought it for her, not liking to appear anywhere with someone not up to his social standing.

"You need to come home and recuperate down south where there are proper doctors and specialists," said her mother, tapping her red lacquered nails on the gleaming wooden table. "I'm positive *this place*"—her emphasis on the last two words was positively dripping with contempt—"wouldn't know a specialist from a podiatrist."

"You would be wrong, Mother," said Lise.

She wasn't the least bit hungry and wouldn't be here at all except for the fact that the two of them appeared at her apartment door half an hour ago. They'd actually taken a taxi from the airport and shown up without calling or texting ahead of time. Quite the military manoeuvre to outflank her ongoing silence in the face of repeated texts and phone calls.

"I didn't agree to this meeting," she said to Aidan, finally looking him square in the eye. "You ambushed me and brought me here, under duress, I might add."

"Oh, Lise! You always exaggerate everything!" exclaimed her mother. "She always did that as a child, too," she said to Aidan. "Making a mountain out of a molehill every chance she could."

"I'm not here because I want to be, *Mother,*" said Lise. "You've both wasted your money—or Aidan's money—flying up here. And I don't exaggerate."

Her mother fluttered both hands at her as if to shove her away and then drank her ice water.

Aidan's eyes gleamed as he stared at her over his menu.

"We're concerned about your welfare. This whole—hostage-taking ordeal—has been all over the national news. Why wouldn't you think your family would want you home?" he said.

"Because my family has no interest in what I want for my life," said Lise as the server approached their table. She shone a smile on the young man, whose name tag read *Reid*. "Hello, I would like the elk stew along with the sourdough bread and a side salad."

"I'll need another minute," Aidan said. "Mom?" he asked Lise's mother, Dorothy.

Mom? Since when has she become your mom?

"Oh, my goodness, don't you have anything on here like chicken? Something normal?" Her mother pretended to fan herself with her menu. "I can't see myself eating anything on here. It's all so *gamey*."

"You're right," said Aidan. "It's all bison and elk and venison." He wrinkled his nose. "I see nothing's changed in the past year and a half. You're eating like the natives."

"Don't eat then," said Lise. "We can all go home sooner. Although, I trust you've booked rooms here? My apartment has only one bed and no pull-out couch."

Her mother hyperventilated. "You are so rude! We fly all the way up here to rescue you and this is how you treat us!"

"Don't need rescuing, and I didn't ask you to come," said Lise. "And besides," she pointed her water glass at Aidan before she took a sip, "I'm sure he's not going to stay in my *decrepit and ancient* apartment."

"I didn't bring you up this way." Dorothy threw her head back as if she was beyond distressed. "I'm so sorry, Aidan. I really don't understand her."

"It's her concussion. She needs to be seen by a proper specialist," declared Aidan. "And I won't rest until she's under the best possible care. If we can't find it in Winnipeg, I'll fly her to Vancouver."

His eyes glittered like a fox's, and she could tell he'd been feeding her mother lies all the way up on the plane. Why this sudden interest in her welfare? Why the sudden fake compassion?

"You both need to order something, or else you'll be sitting here with nothing to do while I eat mine," said Lise as she accepted her fresh mixed salad from Reid with another smile.

"Can I get either of you anything?" asked Reid once again.

"I'll have the vegetable soup," huffed her mother. "There's nothing else on this menu fit for a normal person's stomach."

Aidan glowered at his menu as if the wine and gold-coloured list was a mess of spiders. "I'll have the soup as well," he finally said, "and the bison burger, which I imagine is similar to a regular beef burger?" He put down the menu as if it carried cooties.

Lise rolled her eyes at Reid, not caring what he or anyone else in the restaurant thought of her. These two were embarrassing her, and all she wanted to do was eat and get back home —to her apartment—alone.

"It's similar, yes, sir." Reid gave a little bow, which Lise had never seen him do before. Flustered, the boy headed off to the kitchen with their menus in hand.

"Now," said Aidan, turning the full weight of his attention to Lise. "We need to talk. I realize we didn't leave things... congenially... when you ran back up here and canceled our wedding."

"I canceled our wedding because you thought you could order me around at your whim," Lise ground out. "And because I don't care to be yelled at for the rest of my life."

"Lise, all couples yell from time to time." Her mother actually reached out and patted her hand as if she were a toddler.

"Your dad and I did, too. Couples fight. It's all part of marriage."

"Why did you bring my mother along?" Lise asked Aidan. "Hmm?"

"Your mother and I have watched this brouhaha on the news and know what you've been through…"

"You have no idea what I've been through." Lise's jaw was so tight she was afraid she'd crack a molar. "You have no idea what I do for a living, what my job entails, or why I love it up here. We have nothing to say to each other."

"Your job is not to catch criminals," her mother interjected with a dramatic flair of her hands. "That's for the police. You wanted to work with animals, and here you've been involved in a *shooting*. Lise, you shot a man, don't you understand that?"

Her mother's tomato-red face reminded Lise of the time her parents grounded her for being out past curfew. Right before they kicked her out of the house.

She's really worked up about this, thought Lise as she forked some salad into her mouth and watched her mother's furious eyes. *What's the embarrassing part for her? Because it always came down to whether or not it made the family look bad.*

"We've had our differences, Lise, but that's behind us now." Aidan's voice was velvet as he stroked her other hand. She pulled it away and put it in her lap. "I want to marry you and give you the life you deserve. You don't belong up here." He waved his arm around at the room.

"I know when you come back to Winnipeg, you'll forget all about this, and we can start over. We can rebook The Fairmont Hotel for June, and you will have the wedding of your dreams." Aidan accepted his bowl of soup as Reid served him and then served Dorothy.

"You think so?" said Lise. "You think I can forget that you

get angry on a dime? That I will have no control over my life? Where I go? What I wear?"

"Lise, you're exaggerating again," said her mother.

Lise put up her hand in her mother's face. "That's enough. You love him so much, you marry him. Oh, right. You're already married. Well, I don't love him, and I'm not sticking around to listen to this garbage anymore."

She wiped her mouth with her linen napkin and threw it down on the table. Pushing back her chair, she said, "Book yourselves a couple of rooms here. Fly home tomorrow morning. I'm not coming with you." She pointed at Aidan's face. "And I never want to see you again. Got it?"

People at the surrounding tables sat silent. She knew she was making a scene—the one thing her mother couldn't abide over all other things—but she didn't care. Aidan had brought this on himself. She grabbed her parka from the back of her chair and wove her way among the chairs and tables to the front entrance.

"I'll be back to pay my tab tomorrow," she whispered to the girl on the cash. "Please let Kali know."

The girl simply bobbed her head up and down. Lise drew on her parka and zipped it up. She looked both ways out the front door for bears before she headed to her car parked two spaces down.

A flash of navy-blue parka with a black toque went whizzing around the corner to the side lot. The flash had red hair sticking out of the toque. Only one other person in Churchill had hair that red. Had Rory been inside and heard all of that?

She looked both ways again and didn't see bears or people in either direction. Then, she took off at a run to the side parking lot.

❄

"Rory!" He heard his name but couldn't bring himself to turn around. For crying out loud. How was he supposed to face her? He'd thought he could escape around back and make his way to his truck without being seen.

"Rory, stop!"

Lise was out of breath in the frigid -27C air. She ran up to him and grabbed his arm to physically turn him around. He planted his boots in the snow and shoved his gloved hands into his front parka pockets. His scarf covered the bottom of his face and ears. Lise, as usual, wasn't wearing a toque or scarf.

"You're going to freeze out here. Where's your hat?" he demanded. "Why do you never have a stupid hat on?" His voice was an octave higher than it should have been. How mortifying. Even more mortifying than overhearing the last thing in the world he'd wanted to hear.

"A hat? Who cares? Rory, I left you a couple of phone messages. Why haven't you called me back?" Lise rubbed her mittened hands together and stood rooted in front of him, her skin pinking up from the cold, her beautiful deep blue eyes like gems in the twilight.

"I was... I was going to surprise you," he said.

That sounded lame, so lame. He'd been going to surprise her. He'd gone over to her apartment, and her next-door neighbour told him she was over here. The old lady just left out the minor tidbit that her ex-fiancé and her mother were with her.

"Surprise me how? Never mind..." Lise hugged him even though he stood rigid and didn't remove his hands from his pockets. "What's wrong?" She stared into his eyes, like she was peering into his soul. "What did you hear?"

His tongue stuck to the roof of his mouth. *This is why you stay single,* he admonished himself. *No pain. No worries. No grief.*

"Rory." She shook him. "What did you hear?"

"You're going to have the wedding of your dreams." A crimson flush of anger coursed up his face. He'd walked up to their table in time to see Aidan sliding his finger across the back of her hand and cooing at her about wedding plans.

The female server was going in the opposite direction when he collided with her. He turned so fast to get away that he nearly made himself dizzy.

"What?" She stared at him and shook her head. "No. I'm not. I told him I never want to see him again."

"Yeah. Right." He wished the snow would open up and swallow him right now. Let him die in a frozen tomb and never be found for another thousand years. Scientists could autopsy him and wonder how his heart broke in two. He'd read about people literally dying from broken hearts.

"Rory, I didn't know they were coming. I told him it's over. I never want to see him again."

"He's rich. He can take you to a specialist in Vancouver." He pulled away from her. He couldn't bear to stand this close to her without taking her into his arms, and if he did that, he knew he'd be a goner. A loser. "Wait, did Dr. Stedman say you need to see a specialist?"

"No! Never," she said. "I'm not reading, or on my laptop, or watching the TV. I only turn on the sound because I don't have a radio. I'm following all my concussion protocols."

"Why does he want to take you to Vancouver, then?"

"Because that's Aidan's modus operandi—be the big guy—the flashy guy bossing everyone around," she said, waving her arm. "Not like Joy bosses people. She means well. He does it to control people."

The buzzing in his ears died down, and he realized they

were so close he could count the freckles on her nose. Maybe he did overreact. "I thought you were getting back together."

"He tried to control my every move," she said. "I can't live like that... and... I don't love him." She rocked back on her heels, then took a step back. "Wait, you were supposed to call or text me when you got out of the hospital. How long have you been out?"

"A day or two." He knew he sounded defensive, but so what? He wasn't in a restaurant having dinner with his old love, a fiancé he nearly married. Not to mention a fiancé who'd given him a two-carat pink diamond ring.

"I needed to put the cabin back together. Clean up my watch collection records. Darren stole those watches, and now they're locked up as evidence until his trial."

She looked at him askance as if he wasn't making sense. "Okay," she drew out the word. "I guess I wasn't high on your priority list then."

"Don't be like that..." He was furious with himself. She'd gotten him tongue-tied. Why was talking so easy when they were together on the run? In the hospital?

I'm an idiot. This is stupid.

"We shouldn't be back here. There're bears around," she said. "Why don't you come over for coffee?"

"And meet your old boyfriend?" He was being sarcastic, but it was the only way he knew to protect himself. If he saw that smug jerk, he was likely to break his jaw.

"Rory, come on," she said as he turned away and strode over to his truck parked nearby. He waved at her before he jumped in the driver's seat, fired up the engine, and pulled out of the lot.

She was still standing in the snowy twilight, watching him as he looked in his rearview mirror.

Lone wolf. It's better this way.

CHAPTER 19

One Week Later

Joy appeared on his doorstep holding two enormous paper grocery bags from the Gateway in town. Rory peered through his front window to make sure she was alone and saw his outdoor thermometer read -35 Celsius. She pounded on his wooden door again with her fist.

"Rory, I can see your truck, and I know you're home. Open up."

He padded to the door on sock feet, shoving his hand through his tousled curls. He needed a trim, badly. A good shave up the sides and one of those professional scissor jobs he got every couple of months down in Winnipeg.

Bosco beat him to the door, weaving between his feet and meowing in his squeaky voice.

"What are you doing here?" He waved her into the small foyer. Taking the bags from her, he said, "I have food in the house. Is this from Mom?"

Joy laughed as she shook the snow from her boots. "Urgent

supplies. No, just an excuse to come out on my day off and finally see your place." She toed off her boots and balanced with her hand on his shoulder. "Are you eating anything?" she asked as he headed into the kitchen.

"Of course." He was glad she couldn't see him rolling his eyes. She was in obvious nurse-caretaker mode. "Do you want coffee?"

"Yes, and I'll take a piece of mom's pecan pie while you're at it."

She followed him into the kitchen, turning around and appraising his tidy but rustic wooden cupboards and granite countertop. He'd renovated the cabin himself over the past year and put in a few luxuries.

"Nice place," she finally pronounced. "Beats our rental in town." She sat at the maple table he'd flown up and draped her parka over the back of the chair.

"I have a closet for that," he said, bringing over two coffee mugs. "Sugar? Cream? I can never remember."

"Both, please," she said as she put her hands around her green ceramic mug.

He obliged with cream from the fridge and then pushed the sugar bowl towards her. The pie was on top of the smallest bag of groceries. He made quick work of unpacking everything and then sliced them two large pieces of the pecan pie.

"I don't have any whipped cream," he said. "One of the downfalls of visiting a bachelor." He sat and handed her the pie on matching green plates.

"I'm impressed you've got matching China and cutlery," she joked. "And curtains on the window. Not bad, little brother."

He scrunched up his face at her. "To what do I really owe the pleasure of this visit?"

"You haven't gone back to work yet. I wanted to see how

you're feeling. Dr. Stedman asked me how you were doing, and I was ashamed I didn't know what to say." She dug into her pie but gave him a sharp look over her fork. He could see where Emberlyn had gotten her expressive mahogany brown eyes.

"I'm fine. I wanted some time off."

"No headache? No issues with your heart beating too fast sometimes? Not feeling faint at all?" she asked.

"I told you. I'm fine." He sipped his coffee to buy time from her nosy questions. "I hardly ever take a vacation, so I figured I'd take a week or two."

"Staying holed up in your cabin is hardly a vacation. A vacation from the arctic tundra in November is going to the Bahamas or St. Maarten's."

He made a rude noise. "Heat and sand are over-rated."

"You could go somewhere to ski then," she said, a smile lurking at the corner of her mouth. "You used to love to go on skiing vacations when we were kids."

"Joy, seriously. I just want some peace and quiet."

She licked the back of her fork, her pie demolished. "Okay. I get it. You and Lise went through a terrible ordeal." She reached out and squeezed his free hand. "I'm truly glad you both came home in one piece. And maybe... maybe... you should take some time and talk to someone about it."

He withdrew his hand and crossed his arms with a snort. "Uh-huh. Like a shrink? You think I need to talk to a shrink?"

"They're called psychiatrists, and no, I was thinking more like Gabe Holden, our social worker at the Health Centre. Or, if you think that's too formal, there's always Pastor Stan Gerrard at church." She leaned back in her chair, giving him space, he realized.

"What do you think Pastor Stan could possibly help me with?"

She shrugged. "I don't know. Either of them would be easy

to talk to. You guys were in a life-and-death situation, and that can bring on PTSD. You may not even be aware of the symptoms yet. It's important that you take care of your mental and emotional health as well as your physical health."

"Have you had this little coffee and pie chat with Lise, too?" He sounded like a complete jerk as soon as he said it.

"Actually, yes. She's almost as stubborn as you." Joy smiled. "She at least can admit she's been having nightmares."

"Nightmares? Is she okay?"

"Why don't you ask her?" Joy cocked an eyebrow at him. "She's back at work, but she's struggling. A lot."

"I can't talk to her." He jumped up and poured another cup of coffee from the coffeemaker on the counter. "It would make things worse."

"Only you two know what you went through," said Joy. "I would think you have a lot to talk about."

"I...just stop, okay?" He slammed his mug on the counter, breaking it and spilling coffee everywhere.

Joy jumped up and grabbed a tea towel from the dish rack. "Here, I've got it."

"It's fine!" He whirled around, coffee dripping down his hand and arm. An angry red flush bloomed on his face and headed up into his hairline.

"Rory!" Joy took the broken pieces from him and tossed them into the garbage pail under the sink. "Sit down. Take a breath."

She waited until he finally sat down again and then took both of his hands in hers. She rested her elbows on her thighs and stared him straight in the eyes. "You're my brother, and I love you. Tell me what's going on inside."

His guts were ripping apart. That's what was going on. Emotions were tearing him up and blowing up his head until he couldn't think straight. Blood pounded in his ears, and he turned his head so she couldn't see the unbidden tears that spark in his eyes.

"I couldn't save her," he whispered.

"What?"

"I couldn't save her." His voice broke as he said he tried so hard. "I tried everything, but I couldn't save her."

"Save who? Rory, you saved Lise on the river. If you hadn't gotten there, who knows what would've happened?" Joy leaned forward and gripped his hands tighter. "You saved her in the boat. Don't you remember?"

Single tears left his eyes. They scrunched tight shut as he tried to hold back the flood of emotion. "I failed her completely."

Joy pulled her chair closer till their knees touched, her fingers still entwined in his fingers. "Rory, you didn't fail anybody. You nearly died yourself. Are you having lapses of memory?" She released one hand and brushed his hair to one side of his forehead. "Shhh... it's all right, everything's all right," she whispered.

"Her head disappeared under the water, and I couldn't get to her in time." He cried, huge sobs shaking his shoulders, and Joy drew his head down to her right shoulder.

The warmth of her sweater and the lemon scent of her shampoo enveloped him in safety. He couldn't stop crying as she wrapped her arms around him and gently rocked him in place.

After a long time, Joy put her hands on his cheeks and lifted his head to look at him.

"Rory, Lise was never in the water. She was in the boat. I think you're remembering Dad drowning." Her eyes were soft and loving. He saw compassion and love in them.

"It wasn't your fault, Rory. What happened to Dad was not your fault. It was an accident." She wiped his tears on his cheeks with her thumbs, then let him go as he coughed in embarrassment.

"I lied to Mom." He turned away from her and put his head on the table.

"What do you mean?"

"I told her he had a heart attack. But he tried to save some tourists who panicked when some belugas got too close to their kayaks. They were bashing their paddles in the water, and he capsized. Then he tried to get them to stop when he came back up, but he fell out. I couldn't get to him."

"The coroner still said he drowned, and it was an accident," said Joy.

"Yeah, but I couldn't save him." He shoved away from the table and splashed water on his face at the kitchen sink. "I tried so hard."

"I'm sure you did everything you could, bro. No one blames you, least of all Mom."

"I blame myself," he said, running his hand through his overgrown hair.

"Well, stop it! You've been carrying this all these years? See what I mean? You should've talked to someone about this when it happened."

"Dad would still be here if I'd been quicker or stronger," he argued. "I couldn't paddle fast enough to get there. And then, when I dove for him, I couldn't find him."

"Rory, professional divers couldn't find him. Why did you think you could?"

"You should hate me," he said.

"I do *not* hate you. Not for that, not for anything." Joy tried to hug him, but he evaded her embrace.

"When we were out there... with those criminals," he said, "I asked Lise why she believed God could let terrible things happen to people." He wiped his face with his hand. "She had no idea. Well, I don't know how a so-called loving God could let a good man die for no reason."

"Oh, Rory." Joy gave up trying to hug him and sat down again. "You've been carrying this for so long you're going to burst."

"You got an answer? Because I sure don't." He leaned back against the counter on his hands.

Joy took a deep breath and clasped her hands together, almost as if in prayer.

"You remember the struggles I had with being a single parent and why God let my—relationship—with Emberlyn's father be destroyed." She paused, searching for the right words.

"It led me back to Him. Every hardship I faced, failing out of med school, losing my apartment, it all brought me back to God in a way I'd never experienced Him before then. So, I guess my answer is that God lets bad things happen to teach us to trust Him through the sorrow and difficulties. And to bring us into a closer relationship with Him."

Rory chewed on that in silence. "I haven't felt God in a long time, but when we were out in the cabin with those two criminals, Lise said, 'there're no atheists in foxholes.' And that we were in a foxhole then," he said.

"She was right," said Joy. "And you didn't feel God was with you?"

"I guess I've shut Him out for so long. I wouldn't have recognized Him, anyway."

Joy stood. "Well, I know from all the praying Mom and I did for you guys, God had to be with you. I hope someday you'll realize that, too." She walked over and gave him a hug. He hugged her back.

"Sorry, I'm such a mess."

"You're the best kind of mess," she said, shaking him by the shoulders and smiling.

"What kind is that?" He huffed a laugh.

"The kind that's going to give Lise a call and ask her out for coffee."

He leaned away from her. "Ahh, now..."

"I mean it, bro. She deserves to know you're okay."

"All right." He hugged her again. "Don't be a stranger, eh? Bring Emberlyn out next time and let her play with Bosco."

Joy laughed. "Sure, because then she'll want another cat to go with Domino. If that girl had her way, I would fill the house with every kind of puppy and kitten she sees on TV."

She went and snatched her parka from the back of her chair. "I should run. Don't *you* be a stranger." She headed to the front foyer for her boots. "Mom would love to have us all over for dinner, and that includes Lise, so polish up your best manners and call her."

Rory saluted her as she yanked on her second boot. "Yes, ma'am. I promise I'll call her."

He watched Joy run out to her truck and drive out to the highway. The air was crisp and clear in the deep cold. His body felt light and free. The whirring in his chest was gone.

Who to call first? Lise or Pastor Stan?

Thank You, Lord, for the gift of my sister. Pastor Stan it is.

CHAPTER 20

M*onday, November 21*

Lise stood staring out the living room window of her apartment. She'd shucked off her uniform when she got home for the day and pulled on her favourite cozy sweatsuit from the University of Manitoba. The temperature had stayed level at -32C, and the bears were almost gone from the shoreline. She'd seen a few stragglers on patrol, but they were far from town.

The windswept snowy street before her reminded her she'd made her ultimate break with *home,* as in down south in Winnipeg. She'd arranged with a girlfriend to finally sublet her apartment there, and now there was no going back. She was *here.*

A sharp staccato banging hit her door. Odd, no one had rung the downstairs buzzer. She walked over to check out her peephole in the door. All she could see was the top of a red head of hair. She turned and put her back against the door, her breath caught in her throat.

She hadn't texted him since their parking lot encounter

behind The Great Northern Lodge. She was determined he make the first move. Apparently, he was here, so that must be what was happening. He knocked on the door again, less loudly this time.

Lise opened the door, wishing she'd put on anything besides her sweats and that she'd at least combed her hair before she'd shoved it up on her head in a messy bun. Rory stood in the hallway with two massive brown bags of food, the peppery scent of dinner wafting into her apartment.

"I come in peace," he said, "and I come bearing gifts." A child-like, beseeching look covered his face. He held the bags out towards her like a pizza delivery guy.

"Well, if you brought gifts," she said, opening the door wider, "you'd better come in then."

She stood aside and ushered him past. He entered and put the bags on the counter of her small galley kitchen. The apartment was one main room, cut in half by the kitchen counter, a small bathroom, and the one bedroom off the main room.

He filled the room with his hulking size, and Lise held herself back from hugging him. She would not make a fool out of herself again. He shifted his weight from foot to foot.

"Smells like Ruby's cooking," she offered, finally letting him off the hook in the silence.

"Yeah, have you eaten supper yet?" he asked. "I would've asked you out for dinner, but I thought maybe we could talk better here..."

"I haven't eaten yet, and it smells delicious," she said. "Why don't you hang up your parka, and I'll get some plates?"

She lowered her head as she entered the tiny kitchen. He wanted to talk. Oh man, that was never good. *Here it comes... We need to just be friends... We went through a lot, but there's no need for it to be more than that...*

Lise pulled out two plates and silverware. She grabbed

some napkins and put everything on the countertop. Two stools stood against the opposite side of the counter, as the room was too small for a proper table.

"Here, can you set out the food?" Her voice shook, and she prayed he didn't notice her hands shaking, too. Why would he bring dinner just to talk? Her stomach did a backflip.

"Sure, let me," he said as he expertly flipped open the plastic containers from Ruby's Café and then spooned the contents onto the plates. He sat on the stool and waited for her to come around and sit beside him. "Do you want to say grace?" he asked as she wobbled onto the stool.

"Grace?"

"Yes, bless the food," he said patiently. "Or I can do it."

"You do it," she said in a rush.

He grinned then, the old Rory from their captivity shining through. The Rory who kept her calm, and sane, and safe. She let herself smile back.

"Dear God, bless this food to our use and our bodies to Your service. Amen," he said.

"Amen," she said. "What have we got here?" She picked up her knife and fork and pulled her plate towards her.

"Ruby's Monday night special. Meatloaf, twice-baked potatoes and gravy, and glazed carrots."

"It's perfect. This really hits the spot, thank you," she mumbled through her food.

"My pleasure." He sliced off a piece of meatloaf, and the left side of his mouth quirked up in a grin as he watched her dive into her own plate. "I wasn't sure of the reception I'd get, so I thought it best to bring Mom's home cooking."

"*You* weren't sure?" she said, swallowing the juicy meatloaf and potatoes. "It's been a minute since we last, uh, talked."

"I saw you in church yesterday," Rory said after a pause.

He wiped his hands on his napkin and shifted his bulk on the stool.

"You were in church yesterday?" The shock in her voice permeated the room. "I didn't see you."

"I was in the back, very back row," he admitted. "And it's the first time I've been since I was a teenager."

"Is that what you want to talk about?" Her heart sank, and she mentally chastised herself for her selfishness. She should be thrilled he'd broken down and gone to church. Instead, she'd thought he wanted to talk about *them*. *Them, as in them as a couple.*

"Partly." He cleared his throat. "Pastor Stan's been very helpful. We've met once a week for a bit."

Lise sat back on her stool until she thought she'd fall off. "That's good. It is good, right?"

"Yeah, he's a solid guy. Did you know he leads the AA meeting at the Health Centre?"

"Nope. Don't the leaders have to be recovering alcoholics themselves?" she asked.

"Yeah, he is, so that's why he leads it. He's kind of double-duty pastor." Rory pointed over at her blue plush couch. "Any chance we can talk over there?"

Lise jumped down and headed over to the couch. She plunked down and grabbed a cushion that read 'Boss Lady' and held it in front of her stomach. Whatever was coming, she needed some protection.

Rory perched on the opposite end of the couch, his elbows resting on his knees. If he'd read the words on her pillow, he didn't mention them.

"Listen, I was an idiot…" He stopped. He rubbed his beard scruff. "I shouldn't even have approached your table, knowing you had company. It was rude."

"Company?" She quirked up an eyebrow. "You are always

welcome wherever I am, Rory. After everything we went through, you should know that."

"Well, I shouldn't have reacted that way..." He coughed.

He squirmed in place, and she decided not to let him off the hook. Even though clutching the pillow kept her calm, she waited to see what he'd say without prompting.

"It's just that, what we went through together, I thought maybe... I thought we would..." He stopped and stared at his interlaced fingers.

Silence filled the tiny living room. Lise stared at her wildlife painting of three wolves in the snow over her desk across the room. She needed him to come to whatever this was, or would be, on his own. She knew in her heart she didn't want a man who controlled her, but she also knew she didn't want a man she controlled, either.

The wolves in the painting stared out across the snowy landscape, in front of a stand of black trees. They looked right at her and seemed to say, '*Let him come to you.*'

"I couldn't believe how brave you were through the whole thing, Lise," he finally said, turning to look directly at her. "I couldn't believe how you stood up to Darren and took care of Karl and me and... you did it all."

"I nearly killed you," she said, tears suddenly pooling in her eyes. "I didn't clean your wounds. I just tied you up with that horrible towel."

He shifted towards her and took both hands in his. "You had a lot on your mind, sweetheart. Darren threatened you with a shotgun constantly. He could've killed either of us at any moment. Don't you dare guilt yourself over that for a second."

Her tears fell on their joined hands. "I still can't believe he didn't kill us; you know? It must've been..." She cried harder.

He pulled her into him and put his arms around her. "I believe it was God who was with us all along, just like you said.

There were a lot of people praying for us back here," he said as he rubbed her back.

"You believe in God now?" She inhaled the deep scent of sandalwood and soap on his flannel shirt, even as the shirt muffled her words.

"I think I believed in God all along; I was just angry at God and myself for what happened to my dad," he said, his chin resting on top of her curls. "Pastor Stan and Joy helped me to see it." He kissed the top of her head gently. "And you. You were the first person to challenge my thinking."

He drew back and tilted up her chin. She cursed her tears, but when he wiped them away with his thumb and forefinger, she felt that warmth of safety again. He reached up and softly ran his finger down the scar on her forehead.

"I'm so sorry I let you get hurt," he said. "I'd do anything to do it all over again."

She shook her head. "No, once was more than enough." She gulped on her tears. "Let's agree that we'll never do anything like that again."

She stared into his bright, glowing amber eyes and saw a sheen of tears there as well.

"Never again," he agreed. "There is one more thing…" He brushed her cheek with his right index knuckle and drew his finger under her chin to cup it gently.

"Yes?" she breathed.

He slanted his mouth over hers in a kiss that demanded devotion. His lips, firm and supple, brought her arms around his neck as he explored her lips, bringing shivers to her stomach and knees. His other hand tangled in her hair and shifted to bring her body closer.

When he broke away, he put his forehead on hers and said, "I'm sorry. I didn't mean to go that far."

She bit her bottom lip. "More than friends, right?"

He hugged her tightly to him. "More than friends."

She laughed in relief. "That's the best talk I've ever had."

"Yeah?" He brought his hands down to either side of her neck and chin. "I can't give you two-carat diamonds and condominiums on the ocean."

She cocked an eyebrow at him. "I think I've made it pretty clear that those aren't the things I want."

"What do you want?" He caressed her cheeks with his fingertips. "Are you sure a confirmed bachelor in a cabin who only owns a cat, and a bunch of watches, is what you want?"

She kissed him deeply and without reservation. "That's exactly what I want." She ruffled his hair. "There's two things I love in this world: you and my job." She laughed as a brilliant red flush bloomed on his face. "I knew I had to say it because otherwise, I'd wait forever to hear you say it."

"You've got a lot of confidence in yourself, Officer Dumont," said Rory.

"I have a lot of confidence in the guy who leapt out of his hospital bed to come and save me on a raging river when he was terrified of water," she said.

"Except you didn't need saving," Rory said.

"Yeah, I did." She caressed his beard scruff and smiled. "I was waiting for you."

And she kissed him again as if to hold him forever.

EPILOGUE
ONE YEAR LATER

Rory sat at his desk at home and looked up the number for his watchmaker friend in Winnipeg. The watch his dad had worn on the day he died lay on the desk on a soft piece of suede cloth. The cracked crystal and frozen-in-time hands hadn't changed in seven years, but the strap looked brand new.

He loved that watch. If his mom hadn't given it to him after his dad died, he'd never have started collecting watches. Once he'd begun researching the history of watchmaking, he'd been hooked.

After eight years, it was time to repair his father's watch so he could wear it for himself. He knew his dad would want him to.

Tito and Koko, their twin Yorkies, raced for the door when the doorbell rang. He'd given them to Lise as a wedding present, as well as the new doorbell and security cameras he'd installed after their wedding in January. She didn't mind living twenty-three kilometres out of town, but she'd insisted on a security system.

Rory thought Tito and Koko were the best security system they could have. The dogs sounded like Dobermans and belied their tiny weights of seven and eight pounds, respectively. She adored their sweet, quirky faces and the fact that she could carry both of them draped over one arm.

"I'll get it," she called from the front foyer. Her purple yoga pants and sweatshirt partially hid her six-month-old pregnancy stomach.

"Hey, you're looking great!" The sounds of Kira and Lukas Tanner arriving with their little daughter Sophie filled the cabin.

"Come in, come in," said Lise. She hugged Kira tightly. "Rory, they're here," she called to him.

"I can't wait for this little guy to arrive next week," said Kira as she rubbed her own nine-month-pregnant belly. "He's kicking up quite a ruckus."

Lise and Kira chatted outside his office as Tito and Koko barked and scampered up and down the hallway with Sophie. He sat back and held his father's watch in his hands, the broken crystal glinting in the afternoon light coming through the window.

How he wished his dad was here to meet Lise, and his new grandchild on the way. But God was good. His mother and sister were here to share in the joy of his new family.

I love you, Dad, he thought as he put the watch back in its case for now. *And I'm just saying goodbye for now. I'll see you again someday.*

Rory got up to go greet his friends. He knew his dad would be proud.

ABOUT THE AUTHOR

Laurie Wood is a military spouse, a special needs mom, and confirmed dog lover. She's a member of Sisters in Crime International and serves on the Board of Sisters in Crime Canada West.

Laurie writes both romantic suspense and historical fiction. You can connect with her at her website at https://www.lauriewoodauthor.com.

Manufactured by Amazon.ca
Bolton, ON

36020518R00129